CURIOS

CURIOS

RICHARD MARSH

SOME STRANGE ADVENTURES
OF TWO BACHELORS

Introduction by Karl Wurf.

WILDSIDE PRESS

INTRODUCTION

Richard Marsh was the pseudonym of the English author born Richard Bernard Heldmann (1857–1915). He was born in North London, to lace merchant Joseph Heldmann and Emma Marsh, a lace-manufacturer's daughter.

In his twenties, Heldmann began publishing fiction in magazines, primarily adventure stories for boys, in publications such as *Union Jack*. He became co-editor of *Union Jack*, but was fired after a scandal emerged when he forged cheques in France and England. This crime found him sentenced in 1894 to 18 months' hard labor in an English prison.

After his release, he returned to writing, but had to adopt his now-famous pseudonym, "Richard Marsh," for publication. He never used his real name on work again.

Stories under the Marsh byline began appearing regularly in British magazines in 1888, and his first two novels appeared in 1893. He became a full-time writer and worked until his death of heart disease in 1915. Several novels appeared posthumously.

Although a bestselling author during the late Victorian and Edwardian period, today Heldmann is known primarily for his fine supernatural novel *The Beetle*, first published in 1897—the same year as Bram Stoker's *Dracula*. *The Beetle* was, at first, more popular than *Dracula,* outselling Stoker's classic by a substantial margin. *The Beetle* remained continuously in print until 1960 and has had periodic revivals since then.

Heldmann produced nearly 80 volumes of fiction and numerous short stories in many genres, including horror, crime, romance, and humor. Many of these have been republished in recent years.

Proof that talent runs in families, Marsh's grandson Robert Aickman was himself a notable writer of short "strange stories."

—Karl Wurf
Cabin John, Maryland

THE ADVENTURE OF THE PIPE

(MR. PUGH TELLS THE STORY)

CHAPTER I

THE SMOKING OF THE PIPE

"Randolph Crescent, N.W.

"My dear Pugh,—

"I hope you will like the pipe which I send with this. It is rather a curious example of a certain school of Indian carving, and is a present from

"Yours truly,
"Joseph Tress."

It was really very handsome of Tress—very handsome! The more especially as I was aware that to give presents was not exactly in Tress' line. The truth is that when I saw what manner of pipe it was I was amazed. It was contained in a sandalwood box, which was itself illustrated with some remarkable specimens of carving. I use the word "remarkable" advisedly, because although the workmanship was undoubtedly, in its way, artistic, the result could not be described as beautiful. The carver had thought proper to ornament the box with some of the ugliest figures I remember to have seen. They appeared to me to be devils. Or, perhaps, they were intended to represent deities appertaining to some mythological system with which, thank goodness, I am unacquainted. The pipe itself was worthy of the case in which it was contained. It was of meerschaum, with an amber mouthpiece. It was rather too large for ordinary smoking. But then, of course, one doesn't smoke a pipe like that. There are pipes in my collection which I should as soon think of smoking as I should of eating. Ask a china maniac to let you have afternoon tea out of his Old Chelsea, and you will learn some home truths as to the durability of human friendships. The glory of the pipe, as Tress had suggested, lay in its carving. Not that I claim that it was beautiful, any more than I make such a claim for the carving on the box, but, as Tress said in his note, it was curious.

The stem and the bowl were quite plain, but on the edge of the bowl was perched some kind of lizard. I told myself it was an octopus when I first saw it, but I have since had reason to believe that it was some almost unique member of the lizard tribe. The creature was represented as climbing over the edge of the bowl down towards the stem, and its legs, or feelers, or tentacula, or whatever the things are called, were, if I may use a vulgarism, sprawling about "all over the place." For instance, two or three of them were twined about the bowl, two or three of them were twisted round the stem, and one, a particularly horrible one, was uplifted in the air, so that if you put the pipe in your mouth the thing was pointing straight at your nose.

Not the least agreeable detail about the creature was that it was hideously life-like. It appeared to have been carved in amber, but some colouring matter must have been introduced, for inside the amber the creature was of a peculiarly ghastly green. The more I examined the pipe the more amazed I was at Tress' generosity. He and I are rival collectors. I am not going to say, in so many words, that his collection of pipes contains nothing but rubbish, because, as a matter of fact, he has two or three rather decent specimens. But to compare his collection to mine would be absurd. Tress is conscious of this, and he resents it. He resents it to such an extent that he has been known, at least on one occasion, to declare that one single pipe of his—I believe he alluded to the Brummagem relic preposterously attributed to Sir Walter Raleigh—was worth the whole of my collection put together. Although I have forgiven this, as I hope I always shall forgive remarks made when envious passions get the better of the nobler nature, even of a Joseph Tress, it is not to be supposed that I have forgotten it. He was, therefore, not at all the sort of person from whom I expected to receive a present. And such a present! I do not believe that he himself had a finer pipe in his collection. And to have given it me! I had misjudged the man. I wondered where he had got it from. I had seen his pipes; I knew them off by heart—and some nice trumpery he has among them, too!—but I had never seen *that* pipe before. The more I looked at it, the more my amazement grew. The beast perched upon the edge of the bowl was so life-like. Its two bead-like eyes seemed to gleam at me with positively human intelligence. The pipe fascinated me to such an extent that I actually resolved to—smoke it!

I filled it with Perique. Ordinarily I use bird's-eye, but on those very rare occasions on which I use a specimen I smoke Perique. I lit up with quite a small sensation of excitement. As I did so I kept my eyes perforce fixed upon the beast. The creature pointed its upraised tentacle directly at me. As I inhaled the pungent tobacco, that tentacle impressed me with a feeling of actual uncanniness. It was broad daylight, and I was smoking in front of the window, yet to such an extent was I affected that it seemed to me that the tentacle was not only vibrating, which, owing to the peculiarity of its position, was quite within the range of probability, but actually moving, elongating—stretching forward, that is, further towards me, and towards the tip of my nose. So impressed was I by this idea that I took the pipe out of my mouth, and minutely examined the beast. Really, the delusion was excusable. So cunningly had the artist wrought that he had succeeded in producing a creature which, such was its uncanniness, I could only hope had no original in nature.

Replacing the pipe between my lips, I took several whiffs. Never had smoking had such an effect on me before. Either the pipe, or the creature on it, exercised some singular fascination. I seemed, without an instant's warning, to be passing into some land of dreams. I saw the beast which was perched upon the bowl writhe and twist. I saw it lift itself bodily from the meerschaum....

CHAPTER II

THE MYSTERY OF THE PIPE

"Feeling better now?"

I looked up. Joseph Tress was speaking.

"What's the matter? Have I been ill?"

"You appear to have been in some kind of swoon."

Tress' tone was peculiar, even a little dry.

"Swoon! I never was guilty of such a thing in my life."

"Nor was I, until I smoked that pipe."

I sat up. The act of sitting up made me conscious of the fact that I had been lying down. Conscious, too, that I was feeling more than a little dazed. It seemed as though I was waking out of some strange, lethargic sleep— a kind of feeling which I have read of and heard about, but never before experienced.

"Where am I?"

"You're on a couch in your own room. You *were* on the floor; but I thought it would be better to pick you up and place you on the couch— though no one performed the same kind office to me when I was on the floor."

Again Tress' tone was distinctly dry.

"How came *you* here?"

"Ah, that's the question." He rubbed his chin—a habit of his which has annoyed me more than once before. "Do you think you are sufficiently recovered to enable you to understand a little simple explanation?" I stared at him, amazed. He went on stroking his chin. "The truth is that when I sent you the pipe I made a slight omission."

"An omission?"

"I omitted to advise you not to smoke it."

"And why?"

"Because—well, I've reason to believe the thing is drugged."

"Drugged!"

"Or poisoned."

"Poisoned!" I was wide awake enough then. I jumped off the couch with a celerity which proved it.

"It is this way. I became its owner in rather a singular manner." He paused, as if for me to make a remark; but I was silent. "It is not often that I smoke a specimen, but for some reason, I did smoke this. I commenced to smoke it, that is. How long I continued to smoke it is more than I can say. It had on me the same peculiar effect which it appears to have had on you. When I recovered consciousness I was lying on the floor."

"On the floor?"

"On the floor. In about as uncomfortable a position as you can easily conceive. I was lying face downwards, with my legs bent under me. I was never so surprised in my life as I was when I found myself *where* I was. At first I supposed that I had had a stroke. But by degrees it dawned upon me that I didn't *feel* as though I had had a stroke." (Tress, by the way, has been an army surgeon.) "I was conscious of distinct nausea. Looking about, I saw the pipe. With me it had fallen on to the floor. I took for granted, considering the delicacy of the carving, that the fall had broken it. But when I picked it up I found it quite uninjured. While I was examining it a thought flashed to my brain. Might it not be answerable for what had happened to me? Suppose, for instance, it was drugged? I had heard of such things. Besides, in my case were present all the symptoms of drug-poisoning, though what drug had been used I couldn't in the least conceive. I resolved that I would give the pipe another trial."

"On yourself? Or on another party, meaning me?"

"On myself, dear Pugh—on myself! At that point of my investigations I had not begun to think of you. I lit up and had another smoke."

"With what result?"

"Well, that depends on the standpoint from which you regard the thing. From one point of view the result was wholly satisfactory—I proved that the thing was drugged, and more."

"Did you have another fall?"

"I did. And something else besides."

"On that account, I presume, you resolved to pass the treasure on to me?"

"Partly on that account, and partly on another."

"On my word, I appreciate your generosity. You might have labelled the thing as poison."

"Exactly. But then you must remember how often you have told me that you *never* smoke your specimens."

"That was no reason why you shouldn't have given me a hint that the thing was more dangerous than dynamite."

"That did occur to me afterwards. Therefore I called to supply the slight omission."

"*Slight* omission, you call it! I wonder what you would have called it if you had found me dead."

"If I had known that you *intended* smoking it I should not have been at all surprised if I had."

"Really, Tress, I appreciate your kindness more and more! And where is this example of your splendid benevolence? Have you pocketed it, regretting your lapse into the unaccustomed paths of generosity? Or is it smashed to atoms?"

"Neither the one nor the other. You will find the pipe upon the table. I neither desire its restoration nor is it in any way injured. It is merely an expression of personal opinion when I say that I don't believe that it *could* be injured. Of course, having discovered its deleterious properties, you will not want to smoke it again. You will therefore be able to enjoy the consciousness of being the possessor of what I honestly believe to be the most remarkable pipe in existence. Good-day, Pugh."

He was gone before I could say a word. I immediately concluded, from the precipitancy of his flight, that the pipe *was* injured. But when I subjected it to close examination I could discover no signs of damage. While I was still eyeing it with jealous scrutiny the door opened, and Tress came in again.

"By the way, Pugh, there is one thing I might mention, especially as I know it won't make any difference to you."

"That depends on what it is. If you have changed your mind, and want the pipe back again, I tell you frankly that it won't. In my opinion, a thing once given is given for good."

"Quite so; I don't want it back again. You may make your mind easy upon that point. I merely wanted to tell you *why* I gave it you."

"You have told me that already."

"Only partly, my dear Pugh—only partly. You don't suppose I should have given you such a pipe as that merely because it happened to be drugged? Scarcely! I gave it you because I discovered from indisputable evidence, and to my cost, that it was haunted."

"Haunted?"

"Yes, haunted. Good-day."

He was gone again. I ran out of the room, and shouted after him down the stairs. He was already at the bottom of the flight.

"Tress! Come back! What do you mean by talking such nonsense?"

"Of course it's only nonsense. We know that that sort of thing always is nonsense. But if you should have reason to suppose that there is something in it besides nonsense, you may think it worth your while to make inquiries of me. But I won't have that pipe back again in my possession on any terms—mind that!"

The bang of the front door told me that he had gone out into the street. I let him go. I laughed to myself as I re-entered the room. Haunted! That was not a bad idea of his. I saw the whole position at a glance. The truth of the matter was that he did regret his generosity, and he was ready to go any lengths if he could only succeed in cajoling me into restoring his gift. He was aware that I have views upon certain matters which are not wholly in accordance with those which are popularly supposed to be the views of the day, and particularly that on the question of what are commonly called supernatural visitations I have a standpoint of my own. Therefore it was not a bad move on his part to try to make me believe that about the pipe on which he knew I had set my heart there was something which could not be accounted for by ordinary laws. Yet, as his own sense should have told him it would do, if he had only allowed himself to reflect for a moment, the move failed. Because I am not yet so far gone as to suppose that a pipe, a thing of meerschaum and of amber, in the sense in which I understood the word, *could* be haunted,—a pipe, a mere pipe!

"Holloa! I thought the creature's legs were twined right round the bowl!"

I was holding the pipe in my hand, regarding it with the affectionate eyes with which a connoisseur does regard a curio, when I was induced to make this exclamation. I was certainly under the impression that, when I first took the pipe out of the box, two, if not three, of the feelers had been twined about the bowl—twined *tightly*, so that you could not see daylight between them and it. Now they were almost entirely detached, only the tips touching the meerschaum, and those particular feelers were gathered up as though the creature were in the act of taking a spring. Of course I was under a misapprehension: the feelers *couldn't* have been twined, though, a moment before, I should have been ready to bet a thousand to one that they were. Still, one does make mistakes, and very egregious mistakes, now and then. At the same time, I confess that when I saw that dreadful-looking animal poised on the extreme edge of the bowl, for all the world as though it were just going to spring at me, I was a little startled. I remembered that when I was smoking the pipe I did think I saw the uplifted tentacle moving, as though it were reaching out at me. And I had a clear recollection that just as I had been sinking into that strange state of unconsciousness, I had been under the impression that the creature was writhing and twisting as though it had suddenly become instinct with life. Under the circumstances, these reflections were not pleasant. I wished Tress had not talked that nonsense about the thing being haunted. It was surely sufficient to know that it was drugged and poisonous, without anything else.

I replaced it in the sandalwood box. I locked the box in a cabinet. Quite apart from the question as to whether that pipe was or was not haunted, I know it haunted me. It was with me, in a figurative—which was worse than an actual—sense, all the day. Still worse, it was with me all the night. It was with me in my dreams. Such dreams! Possibly I had not yet wholly recovered from the effects of that insidious drug, but, whether or no, it was very wrong of Tress to set my thoughts into such a channel. He knows that I am of a highly imaginative temperament, and that it is easier to get morbid thoughts into my mind than to get them out again. Before that night was through I wished very heartily that I had never seen the pipe! I woke from one nightmare to fall into another. One dreadful dream was with me all the time—of a hideous, green reptile which advanced towards me out of some awful darkness, slowly, inch by inch, until it clutched me round the neck, and, glueing its lips to my throat, sucked the life's blood out of my veins, as it embraced me, with a slimy hiss. Such dreams are not restful. I woke anything but refreshed when the morning came. And when I got up and dressed I felt that, on the whole, it would perhaps have been better if I never had gone to bed. My nerves were unstrung, and I had that generally tremulous feeling which is, I believe, an inseparable companion of the more advanced stages of dipsomania. I ate no breakfast. I am no breakfast eater as a rule, but that morning I ate absolutely nothing.

"If this sort of thing is to continue, I will let Tress have his pipe again. He may have the laugh of me, but anything is better than this."

It was with almost funereal forebodings that I went to the cabinet in which I had placed the sandalwood box. But when I opened it my feelings of gloom partially vanished. Of what phantasies had I been guilty! It must have been an entire delusion on my part to have supposed that those tentacula had ever been twined about the bowl. The creature was in exactly the same position in which I had left it the day before—as, of course, I knew it would be!—poised, as if about to spring. I was telling myself how foolish I had been to allow myself to dwell for a moment on Tress' words, when Martin Brasher was shown in.

Brasher is an old friend of mine. We have a common ground—ghosts. Only we approach them from different points of view. He takes the scientific—psychological—inquiry side. He is always anxious to hear of a ghost, so that he may have an opportunity of "showing it up."

"I've something in your line here," I observed, as he came in.

"In my line? How so? *I'm* not pipe mad."

"No, but you're ghost mad. And this is a haunted pipe."

"A haunted pipe! I think you're rather more mad about ghosts, my dear Pugh, than I am."

Then I told him all about it. He was deeply interested, especially when I told him that the pipe was drugged. But when I repeated Tress' words about its being haunted, and mentioned my own delusion about the creature moving, he took a more serious view of the case than I had expected he would do.

"I propose that we act on Tress' suggestion, and go and make inquiries of him."

"But you don't really think that there is anything in it?"

"On these subjects I never allow myself to think at all. There are Tress' words, and there is your story. It is agreed on all hands that the pipe has peculiar properties. It seems to me that there is a sufficient case here to merit inquiry."

He persuaded me. I went with him. The pipe in the sandalwood box went too. Tress received us with a grin—a grin which was accentuated when I placed the sandalwood box upon the table.

"You understand," he said, "that a gift is a gift. On no terms will I consent to receive that pipe back in my possession."

I was rather nettled by his tone.

"You need be under no alarm. I have no intention of suggesting anything of the kind."

"Our business here," began Brasher—I must own that his manner is a little ponderous—"is of a scientific, I may say also, and at the same time, of a judicial nature. Our object is the Pursuit of Truth and the Advancement of Inquiry."

"Have you been trying another smoke?" inquired Tress, nodding his head towards me.

Before I had time to answer Brasher went droning on:—

"Our friend here tells me that you say this pipe is haunted."

"I say it is haunted because it is haunted."

I looked at Tress. I half suspected that he was poking fun at us. But he appeared to be serious enough.

"In these matters," remarked Brasher, as though he were giving utterance to a new and important truth, "there is a scientific and a non-scientific method of inquiry. The scientific method is to begin at the beginning. May I ask how this pipe came into your possession?"

Tress paused before he answered.

"You may ask." He paused again. "Oh, you certainly may ask. But it doesn't follow that I shall tell you."

"Surely your object, like ours, can be but the Spreading About of the Truth?"

"I don't see it at all. It is possible to imagine a case in which the spreading about of the truth might make me look a little awkward."

"Indeed!" Brasher pursed up his lips. "Your words would almost lead one to suppose that there was something about your method of acquiring the pipe which you have good and weighty reasons for concealing."

"I don't know why I should conceal the thing from you. I don't suppose either of you is any better than I am. I don't mind telling you how I got the pipe. I stole it."

"Stole it!"

Brasher seemed both amazed and shocked. But I, who had had previous experience of Tress' methods of adding to his collection, was not at all surprised. Some of the pipes which he calls his, if only the whole truth about them were publicly known, would send him to jail.

"That's nothing!" he continued. "All collectors steal! The eighth commandment was not intended to apply to them. Why, Pugh there has 'conveyed' three-fourths of the pipes which he flatters himself are his."

I was so dumbfounded by the charge that it took my breath away. I sat in astounded silence. Tress went raving on:—

"I was so shy of this particular pipe when I had obtained it, that I put it away for quite three months. When I took it out to have a look at it something about the thing so tickled me that I resolved to smoke it. Owing to peculiar circumstances attending the manner in which the thing came into my possession, and on which I need not dwell—you don't like to dwell on those sort of things, do you, Pugh?—I knew really nothing about the pipe. As was the case with Pugh, one peculiarity I learned from actual experience. It was also from actual experience that I learned that the thing was—well, I said haunted, but you may use any other word you like."

"Tell us, as briefly as possible, what it was you really did discover."

"Take the pipe out of the box!" Brasher took the pipe out of the box and held it in his hand. "You see that creature on it. Well, when I first had it it was underneath the pipe."

"How do you mean that it was underneath the pipe?"

"It was bunched together underneath the stem, just at the end of the mouthpiece, in the same way in which a fly might be suspended from the ceiling. When I began to smoke the pipe I saw the creature move."

"But I thought that unconsciousness immediately followed."

"It did follow, but not before I saw that the thing was moving. It was because I thought that I had been, in a way, a victim of delirium that I tried the second smoke. Suspecting that the thing was drugged I swallowed what I believed would prove a powerful antidote. It enabled me to resist the influence of the narcotic much longer than before, and while I still retained my senses I saw the creature crawl along under the stem, and over the bowl. It was that sight, I believe, as much as anything else, which sent me silly. When I came to again I then and there decided to present the pipe to Pugh. There is one more thing I would remark. When the pipe left me the creature's legs were twined about the bowl. Now they are withdrawn. Possibly you, Pugh, are able to cap my story with a little one which is all your own."

"I certainly did imagine that I saw the creature move. But I supposed that while I was under the influence of the drug imagination had played me a trick."

"Not a bit of it! Depend upon it, the beast is bewitched. Even to my eye it looks as though it were, and to a trained eye like yours, Pugh! You've been looking for the devil a long time, and you've got him at last."

"I—I wish you wouldn't make those remarks, Tress. They jar on me."

"I confess," interpolated Brasher—I noticed that he had put the pipe down on the table as though he were tired of holding it—"that to *my* thinking, such remarks are not appropriate. At the same time what you have told us, is, I am bound to allow, a little curious. But of course what I require is ocular demonstration. I haven't seen the movement myself."

"No but you very soon will do if you care to have a pull at the pipe on your own account. Do, Brasher, to oblige me! There's a dear!"

"It appears then, that the movement is only observable when the pipe is smoked. We have at least arrived at step No. 1."

"Here's a match, Brasher. Light up, and we shall have arrived at step No. 2."

Tress lit a match, and held it out to Brasher. Brasher retreated from his neighbourhood.

"Thank you, Mr. Tress, I am no smoker, as you are aware. And I have no desire to acquire the art of smoking by means of a poisoned pipe."

Tress laughed. He blew out the match and threw it into the grate.

"Then I tell you what I'll do—I'll have up Bob."

"Bob? Why Bob?"

"Bob"—whose real name was Robert Haines, though I should think he must have forgotten the fact, so seldom was he addressed by it—was Tress' servant. He had been an old soldier, and had accompanied his master when he left the service. He was as depraved a character as Tress himself. I am not sure even that he was not worse than his master. I shall never forget how he once behaved towards myself. He actually had the assurance to accuse *me* of attempting to steal the Wardour Street relic which Tress fondly deludes himself was once the property of Sir Walter Raleigh. The truth is that I had slipped it with my pocket-handkerchief into my pocket in a fit of absence of mind. A man who could accuse me of such a thing would be guilty of anything. I was therefore quite at one with Brasher when he asked what Bob could possibly be wanted for. Tress explained.

"I'll get him to smoke the pipe," he said.

Brasher and I exchanged glances, but we refrained from speech.

"It won't do him any harm," said Tress.

"What—not a poisoned pipe?" asked Brasher.

"It's not poisoned—it's only drugged."

"*Only* drugged!"

"Nothing hurts Bob. He is like an ostrich. He has digestive organs which are peculiarly his own. It will only serve him as it served me—and Pugh—it will knock him over. It is all done in the Pursuit of Truth and for the Advancement of Inquiry."

I could see that Brasher did not altogether like the tone in which Tress repeated his words. As for myself, it was not to be supposed that I should put myself out in a matter which in no way concerned me. If Tress chose to poison the man, it was his affair, not mine. He went to the door, and shouted:—

"Bob! Come here, you scoundrel!"

That is the way in which he speaks to him. No really decent servant would stand it. I shouldn't dare to address Nalder, my servant, in such a way. He would give me notice on the spot. Bob came in; he is a great hulking fellow, who is always on the grin. Tress had a decanter of brandy in his hand. He filled a tumbler with the neat spirit.

"Bob, what would you say to a glassful of brandy—the real thing, my boy?"

"Thank you, sir."

"And what would you say to a pull at a pipe when the brandy is drunk?"

"A pipe?" The fellow is sharp enough when he likes. I saw him look at the pipe upon the table and then at us, and then a gleam of intelligence came into his eyes. "I'd do it for a dollar, sir."

"A dollar, you thief?"

"I meant ten shillings, sir."

"Ten shillings, you brazen vagabond?"

"I should have said a pound."

"A pound! Was ever the like of that? Do I understand you to ask a pound for taking a pull a your master's pipe?"

"I'm thinking that I'll have to make it two."

"The deuce you are! Here, Pugh, lend me a pound."

"I'm afraid I've left my purse behind."

"Then lend me ten shillings—Ananias!"

"I doubt if I have more than five."

"Then give me the five. And Brasher, lend me the other fifteen."

Brasher lent him the fifteen. I doubt if we shall either of us ever see our money again. He handed the pound to Bob.

"Here's the brandy—drink it up." Bob drank it without a word, draining the glass of every drop. "And here's the pipe."

"Is it poisoned, sir?"

"Poisoned, you villain! What do you mean?"

"It isn't the first time I've seen your tricks, sir—is it now? And you're not the one to give a pound for nothing at all. If it kills me you'll send my body to my mother—she'd like to know that I was dead."

"Send your body to your grandmother! You idiot, sit down and smoke!"

Bob sat down. Tress had filled the pipe, and handed it, with a lighted match, to Bob. The fellow declined the match. He handled the pipe very gingerly, turning it over and over, eyeing it with all his eyes.

"Thank you, sir—I'll light up myself if it's the same to you. I carry matches of my own. It's a beautiful pipe, entirely. I never see the like of it for ugliness. And what's the slimy-looking varmint that looks as though it would like to have my life? Is it living, or is it dead?"

"Come, we don't want to sit here all day, my man."

"Well, sir, the look of this here pipe has quite upset my stomach. I'd like another drop of liquor, if it's the same to you."

"Another drop! Why, you've had a tumblerful already! Here's another tumblerful to put on top of that. You won't want the pipe to kill you—you'll be killed before you get to it."

"And isn't it better to die a natural death?"

Bob emptied the second tumbler of brandy as though it were water. I believe he would empty a hogshead without turning a hair! Then he gave another look at the pipe. Then, taking a match from his waistcoat-pocket, he drew a long breath, as though he were resigning himself to fate. Striking the match on the seat of his trousers, while, shaded by his hand, the flame was gathering strength, he looked at each one of us in turn. When he looked at Tress I distinctly saw him wink his eye. What my feelings would have been if a servant of mine had winked his eye at me I am unable to imagine! The match was applied to the tobacco, a puff of smoke came through his lips—the pipe was alight!

During this process of lighting the pipe we had sat—I do not wish to use exaggerated language, but we had sat and watched that alcoholic scamp's proceedings as though we were witnessing an action which would leave its mark upon the age. When we saw that the pipe was lighted we gave a simultaneous start. Brasher put his hands under his coat-tails and gave a kind of hop. I raised myself a good six inches from my chair, and Tress rubbed his palms together with a chuckle. Bob alone was calm.

"Now," cried Tress, "you'll see the devil moving."

Bob took the pipe from between his lips.

"See what?" he said.

"Bob, you rascal, put that pipe back into your mouth, and smoke it for your life!"

Bob was eyeing the pipe askance.

"I dare say, but what I want to know is whether this here varmint's dead or whether he isn't. I don't want to have him flying at my nose—and he looks vicious enough for anything."

"Give me back that pound, you thief, and get out of my house, and bundle."

"I ain't going to give you back no pound."

"Then smoke that pipe!"

"I am smoking it, ain't I?"

With the utmost deliberation Bob returned the pipe to his mouth. He emitted another whiff or two of smoke.

"Now—now!" cried Tress all excitement, and wagging his hand in the air.

We gathered round. As we did so Bob again withdrew the pipe.

"What is the meaning of all this here? I ain't going to have you playing none of your larks on me. I know there's something up, but I ain't going to throw my life away for twenty shillings—not quite, I ain't."

Tress, whose temper is not at any time one of the best, was seized with quite a spasm of rage.

"As I live, my lad, if you try to cheat me by taking that pipe from between your lips until I tell you, you leave this room that instant, never again to be a servant of mine."

I presume the fellow knew from long experience when his master meant what he said and when he didn't. Without an attempt at remonstrance, he replaced the pipe. He continued stolidly to puff away. Tress caught me by the arm.

"What did I tell you? There—there! That tentacle is moving."

The uplifted tentacle *was* moving. It was doing what I had seen it do, as I supposed, in my distorted imagination—it was reaching forward. Undoubtedly Bob saw what it was doing; but, whether in obedience to his master's commands, or whether because the drug was already beginning to take effect, he made no movement to withdraw the pipe. He watched the slowly advancing tentacle, coming closer and closer towards his nose, with an expression of such intense horror on his countenance that it became quite shocking. Further and further the creature reached forward, until on a sudden, with a sort of jerk, the movement assumed a downward direction, and the tentacle was slowly lowered until the tip rested on the stem of the pipe. For a moment the creature remained motionless. I was quieting my nerves with the reflection that this thing was but some trick of the carver's art, and that what we had seen we had seen in a sort of nightmare, when the whole hideous reptile was seized with what seemed to be a fit of convulsive shuddering. It seemed to be in agony. It trembled so violently that I expected to see it loosen its hold of the stem and fall to the ground. I was sufficiently master of myself to steal a glance at Bob. We had had an inkling of what might happen. He was wholly unprepared. As he saw that dreadful inhuman-looking creature, coming to life as it seemed, within an inch or two of his nose, his eyes dilated to twice their usual size. I hoped, for his sake, that unconsciousness would supervene through the action of the drug, before, through sheer fright, his senses left him. Perhaps mechanically, he puffed steadily on.

The creature's shuddering became more violent. It appeared to swell before our eyes. Then, just as suddenly as it began, the shuddering ceased. There was another instant of quiescence. Then—the creature began to crawl along the stem of the pipe! It moved with marvellous caution, the merest fraction of an inch at a time. But still it moved! Our eyes were riveted on it with a fascination which was absolutely nauseous. I am unpleasantly affected even as I think of it now. My dreams of the night before had been nothing to this.

Slowly, slowly, it went, nearer and nearer to the smoker's nose. Its mode of progression was in the highest degree unsightly. It glided—never, so far as I could see, removing its tentacles from the stem of the pipe. It slipped its hindmost feelers onward, until they came up to those which were in advance. Then, in their turn, it advanced those which were in front. It seemed, too, to move with the utmost labour, shuddering as though it were in pain.

We were all, for our parts, speechless. *I* was momentarily hoping that the drug would take effect on Bob. Either his constitution enabled him to offer a strong resistance to narcotics, or else the large quantity of neat spirit which he had drunk acted—as Tress had malevolently intended that it should do—as an antidote. It seemed to me that he would *never* succumb. On went the creature—on and on, in its infinitesimal progression. I was spellbound. I would have given the world to scream, to have been able to utter a sound. I could do nothing else but watch.

The creature had reached the end of the stem. It had gained the amber mouthpiece. It was within an inch of the smoker's nose. Still on it went.

It seemed to move with greater freedom on the amber. It increased its rate of progress. It was actually touching the foremost feature on the smoker's countenance. I expected to see it grip the wretched Bob, when it began to oscillate from side to side. Its oscillations increased in violence. It fell to the floor. That same instant the narcotic prevailed. Bob slipped sideways from the chair, the pipe still held tightly between his rigid jaws.

We were silent. There lay Bob. Close beside him lay the creature. A few more inches to the left, and he would have fallen on and squashed it flat. It had fallen on its back. Its feelers were extended upwards. They were writhing and twisting and turning in the air.

Tress was the first to speak.

"I think a little brandy wouldn't be amiss." Emptying the remainder of the brandy into a glass, he swallowed it at a draught. "Now for a closer examination of our friend." Taking a pair of tongs from the grate he nipped the creature between them. He deposited it upon the table. "I rather fancy that this is a case for dissection."

He took a penknife from his waistcoat-pocket. Opening the large blade, he thrust its point into the object on the table. Little or no resistance seemed to be offered to the passage of the blade, but as it was inserted, the tentacula simultaneously began to writhe and twist. Tress withdrew the knife.

"I thought so!" He held the blade out for our inspection. The point was covered with some viscid-looking matter. "That's blood! The thing's alive!"

"Alive!"

"Alive! That's the secret of the whole performance!"

"But—"

"But me no buts, my Pugh! The mystery's exploded! One more ghost is lost to the world! The person from whom I *obtained* that pipe was an Indian juggler—up to many tricks of the trade. He, or some one for him, got hold of this sweet thing in reptiles—and a sweeter thing would, I imagine, be hard to find—and covered it with some preparation of, possibly, gum arabic. He allowed this to harden. Then he stuck the thing—still living, for those sort of gentry are hard to kill—to the pipe. The consequence was that when any one lit up the warmth was communicated to the adhesive agent—again some preparation of gum, no doubt—it moistened it, and the creature, with infinite difficulty, was able to move. But I am open to lay odds with any gentleman of sporting tastes that *this* time the creature's travelling days *are* done. It has given me rather a larger taste of the horrors than is good for my digestion."

With the aid of the tongs he removed the creature from the table. He placed it on the hearth. Before Brasher or I had a notion of what it was he intended to do he covered it with a heavy marble paper-weight. Then he stood upon the weight, and between the marble and the hearth he ground the creature flat.

While the execution was still proceeding, Bob sat up upon the floor.

"Holloa!" he asked—"what's happened?"

"We've emptied the bottle, Bob," said Tress. "But there's another where that came from. Perhaps you could drink another tumblerful, my boy?"

Bob drank it!

THE ADVENTURE OF
THE PHONOGRAPH

(MR. TRESS TELLS THE STORY)

CHAPTER I

THE DISCOVERY OF THE VOICE

"Well, Pugh, what is the latest thing in playthings?"

I had entered the room unnoticed, and for a second or two had been standing at the door watching him. He was seated at a table with, in front of him, what seemed to be an oblong mahogany box. In one hand he had a long flexible tube, the two ends of which he was holding to his ears. So engrossed was he with his occupation that he had not been conscious of my entrance. At the sound of my voice he dropped the tube, and sprang to his feet with what seemed to me to be unnecessary noise and clatter.

"Tress—Good gracious! How you startled me!"

He did seem startled. He was actually trembling. His eyes stared at me from behind his glasses as if they had been staring at a spectre. He caught at the back of a chair, as if desirous of its support to conceal his agitation. I was conscious that Pugh was a poor, nerveless creature. I supposed that his obvious discomposure was caused by my sudden interruption. Paying no heed to it, I advanced to the table. I laid my hand upon the box.

"What's this?"

"That!" Pugh was still glaring at me as if I were a ghost. He spoke with a little gasp: "That's a phonograph."

It may seem odd, but I suppose there are a good many people—decent, respectable people—who never have seen a phonograph; at any rate, until that moment I had been one of them. I had had no idea what the thing looked like. I regarded its exterior with curiosity. While I was doing so Pugh regarded me. Presently he laid his hand upon my arm; a perceptible tremor was in his voice.

"Tress, a most extraordinary thing has happened. I am glad that you have come. You may be able to suggest something which will relieve my mind. It has made me most uncomfortable."

"It doesn't take much to do that, does it, Pugh?"

"Don't gibe at me; at least, until you know what you are gibing at. Sit down and listen."

"Listen to what?"

"To the voice of the phonograph."

Pugh's own voice was solemn enough—almost funereal. I did as he bade me. I sat down; I inserted the two ear-pieces in my ears; Pugh touched what I took to be some sort of a handle; the machine was set in motion; and I listened.

He might have told me what it was I might expect to hear. It must be remembered—I repeat it—that that was my first introduction to the phonograph; the result of the introduction was, I confess, to startle me. I heard, as clearly as if she were speaking within a foot of where I was sitting, a woman's voice. Although it was unmistakably a woman's voice, it was marked by some curious qualities. It was as though she were speaking in a condition of acute nervous tension; as if she were pressed for time. The utterance, though distinct, was hurried. The tone, firm at first, all at once became marked by a note of fear—all the more marked because obviously restrained. Immediately afterwards the whole fashion of the voice was changed—it became a shrill screech of agonising terror. It was punctuated by shrieks, involuntary shrieks, because through them, as it were, the woman still struggled to speak. With them were mingled faint sounds, as of a struggle, and of blows; an occasional murmur of a man's voice; on a sudden, the man's voice burst into a wild roar of savage rage; shriek after shriek from the woman; an odd swishing sound, as of a current of air, a dull thud; and the phonograph was still.

I own, as I have said, that I was startled. I take it that any man who had made his first acquaintance with a phonograph under similar circumstances would have been startled too. I put down the ear-pieces. I looked at the machine. I looked at Pugh.

"This is a pretty sort of plaything, upon my word! You seem to have brought the Theatre of Horrors, Whitechapel, into your own home."

"You heard it?"

"Heard it! I should think I did. I seem to have seen it, too. I almost feel as if I had been the cold-blooded witness of a murder, or of something very like one."

Pugh's answer took me aback. He leaned over the machine. He peered at me through his spectacles.

"Suppose we have?"

"Suppose we have what?"

"Suppose we have, in a sense, been the witnesses—one might almost say the supernatural witnesses—of a dreadful crime?"

"What the dickens do you mean?"

"I will tell you."

He sat down. His lips were quivering. He fixed his spectacles upon his nose, with a hand which shook. His agitation had evidently not diminished. I began to have an inkling of the cause of it. It was with an obvious effort that he told his tale.

"I have just brought the phonograph home with me, perhaps half an hour before you came. I saw it in the window of a pawnbroker's shop in the Fulham Road. The notice, 'A phonograph to be sold cheap,' caught my eye. I went in and bought it. There are twelve cylinders which go with it—here they are."

Pugh drew my attention to a box which he had placed behind the phonograph upon the table.

"I understood the shop assistant to say that the machine had belonged to a man who used it for exhibition purposes. Nine of the cylinders have records—you see, they are labelled."

He held them out for me to see. He read the labels which were affixed to them:—

"'Military Band,' 'My Old Dutch,' 'Home, Sweet Home,' 'Pianoforte Solo,' and all the rest of it. I suppose you paid your penny, or whatever it was, and took your choice of which you wished to hear. Two of the cylinders are blank. The twelfth, which you have listened to, is now in the machine—unlabelled."

"Well?"

For Pugh had paused, as if he thought that he had made a point.

"What of that? For some reason or other the man omitted to label it, that is all."

"That may be the reason, or"—Pugh's tone became a whisper—"there may be another. Listen, Tress, to the other records, and then to this again, and then tell me if the same dreadful thought which has occurred to me does not occur to you—at least, as being within the range of possibility."

"I have no objection. I will listen to the lot of them with pleasure. To me a phonograph is what a new toy is to a child—a pleasing novelty."

I listened. I heard what, I suppose, were meant for comic songs, shouted by hoarse voices, and sentimental songs shrieked by shrill ones. I heard, first, what seemed to be a German band, and then a piano, which badly wanted tuning, grind out "variations" on "popular airs." And I heard other things. It was all very curious, no doubt, but I do not know that it was particularly impressive. And then there came again the sound of the woman's voice. After what had gone before, it came with something of the nature of a shock. The force of the contrast heightened the effect. Certainly, anything more realistic I had never heard. It was the sense of reality, of propinquity, which so affected one. I admit that I was impressed the second time of hearing to the full as much as I had been the first. I found it difficult not to believe that I had been listening to that woman's shrieks of agony in some sort of dreadful waking dream. Pugh sat and watched me, reading in my countenance, I have no doubt, something of what I felt.

"Isn't there a difference between the comic songs and the sentimental songs and that?"

"My dear Pugh, there's all the difference in the world."

"I tell you what we'll do. You listen again, and tell me what she says, and I'll take it down from your dictation."

I acted on his suggestion. He got out a sheet of paper and a pencil. As I listened, I repeated to him aloud what the woman said to me out of the heart of the phonograph. When the voice was still, this, according to Pugh's report, was what the woman had said:—

"My name is Jane Clinch. My husband is mad drunk. He has locked me in the room with him. I can't get out. He is going to kill me. He doesn't know what he is doing. He's sharpening his knife. He's got a hammer. They're not to hang him. My husband's mad. He's good to me when he's sober; he's always good. Oh—he's coming!"

Here the voice, speaking from the phonograph, changed its character entirely; it became instinct with wild, unreasoning terror:—

"Don't, Jack! Don't! oh—oh!" Shriek followed shriek. "Not the knife, Jack! not the knife!"

There were sounds without words, as if the woman had been dragged away from the near neighbourhood of the instrument, and, in consequence it had only been able to register fragments of the words she uttered. The fragments were mingled with screams—screams which made one's blood run cold—and with sounds which were hideously suggestive of blows struck with insensate violence. Now and then one heard a man's voice, hoarse with frenzy. What it was he said it was impossible to make out, but the tone was eloquent. Then the woman's voice broke again into articulate speech—such speech!—

"He's killing me! he's killing me!"

There came an ear-splitting yell, immediately followed by a husky roar from the man:

"*Damn you, take that!*"

A heavy thud, and all was still.

When I had got to the end of what Pugh had written, we sat for some moments in silence. Reading the written words was sufficiently gruesome; listening to them had been much worse. No mere description could give an adequate idea of the horror of them, as they proceeded from the interior of that thing of wood and wax and metal. Pugh broke the silence:—

"What do you make of it?"

"I don't know what to make of it. If that was intended for a penny-worth, I should think that it was considered good value by those who paid their pennies. A trifle lurid, perhaps, but satisfying."

"I doubt if it was ever intended for a pennyworth. Listen to me, Tress. This phonograph belonged to a man who used it to gain a livelihood. He would not have sold it unless urged by dire necessity. Might not drink have been his ruin? Can you not conceive of him as a wretched drunkard, with a helpless wife? In a fit of sudden delirium he resolves to murder her. She is alone in the room with him. He locks the door. Cut off from succour, conscious of her danger, her reasoning faculties half paralysed by terror, she forms a wild determination to make of the phonograph her confidant. He attacks her while in the act of doing so. Can there be any doubt that it is because the woman has been dragged away from the instrument that the registration of her words is here and there imperfect? She makes a frantic rush to get back at it. She screams, 'He is killing me!' and, while the words still are trembling on her lips, the miscreant slays her. What else can be the meaning of his savage exclamation, 'Take that!' and of the dreadful thud which follows?"

Pugh came closer to me. He lowered his voice:—

"Is it not possible that that unfortunate woman, Jane Clinch, has handed down, unto eternity, an actual record of her last moments—an undying witness of her awful end? The phonograph has confided to us its terrible secret. On us may be laid the task of becoming the avengers of innocent blood."

I had always been aware that there was in Pugh a vein of what he calls romance, and of what I call drivel. But I had not hitherto credited him with sufficient ingenuity to build up so plausible a theory upon so small a basis of fact. For the theory was plausible—that was the point of it.

"You missed your vocation, my dear Pugh, in not adopting fiction as your profession. There is only one little detail required to make your fiction fact; that is, proof of any sort that a woman named Jane Clinch has been murdered. Do you happen to have seen anything about it in the papers?"

"Nothing; but that is immaterial." Rising from his chair, Pugh began to pace about the room. "Many undiscovered crimes lie hidden in this great city. I shall make it my business to watch the papers, to search the records of the police courts, of the station-houses. If nothing is to be learned from such sources, I may think it my duty to advertise for information of a woman named Jane Clinch. In that way, possibly, the mystery may be unfolded. I feel"—turning, Pugh pointed at the phonograph with a gesture which no doubt he intended to be impressive—"I feel that by means of that phonograph a voice has spoken to me from beyond the confines of the grave. It has made to me an appeal which I dare not allow to remain unanswered."

"All right," I said. "Then answer it."

He did, the very next day.

CHAPTER II

THE DISCOVERY OF THE MAN

I was examining, through a microscope, a fine intaglio which I had picked up for a song from a man in the neighbourhood of the docks—I have picked up some of the best things I have within a three-mile walk of the other side of Tower Hill—when Pugh came in. He was carrying a newspaper in his hand. I could see at once from his manner that his mind was "big with the fate of Rome."

"Tress," he began—blurting out without an instant's loss of time the errand he had come upon—"I've found Jane Clinch!"

"Jane Clinch?" I had to consider for a second to whom he was alluding. I had not been thinking of nothing else since yesterday. Then I remembered. "Do you mean the woman of the phonograph?"

"Precisely! The woman of the phonograph. I have found her!"

"You don't say so! Dead or alive?"

"Dead, Tress, dead! Foully done to death! This event is likely to prove historical. We have arrived at a new epoch in the discovery of crime. For the first time the phonograph has acted as a detective."

"Indeed!" Pugh's excitement was a little too much for me. "I don't know that I am interested in Jane Clinch, or in new epochs in the discovery of crime, so perhaps you'll explain. I'm dusting my intaglios; here's a fine one which I only bought last week—just look at it!"

He pretended not to be interested. Whenever I make a remarkable addition to my collection, the man's jealousy is crass.

"How can you talk of trifles in the presence of such an event as this?" He slapped his hand down on to the newspaper he was holding. "Tress, for shame!" As usual, Pugh was becoming more than a little absurd. "Read that."

He handed me the paper, pointing with his finger as he did so to a particular paragraph. It was headed, "Shocking Discovery in South Lambeth." To a public surfeited with horrors, its purport was sufficiently commonplace. The body of a woman had been found stowed away in an egg-box, under an arch somewhere in Lambeth. What the discovery had to do with Jane Clinch I failed to see. I said so.

"Don't you see that her linen was marked 'J. C.'?"

"Well? Her name might have been Jemima Caudle, for all you know."

"It might have been, but it was not. That woman is Jane Clinch; something tells me so. True, I am not as yet in a position to prove it, but I quickly will be. I have just come from the pawnbroker from whom I bought the phonograph. I wanted to learn some particulars of the man who originally sold it. The fellow had been to the shop only a few minutes before I got there, wanting to buy it back again."

"That doesn't look as if he had a guilty conscience."

"Doesn't it? To me, that is exactly what it does look like. My theory is this. The fellow sold it in order to get drink, to enable him at any price to drown the memory of his crime; the shop assistant owns that he looked like a man who drank heavily. As soon as he had sold it, he remembers, hazily, how the victim of his madness strove to make of it her confidant. He is haunted by the fear that it may contain some fatal testimony of his guilt. He feels that, at all and every risk, he must get it back again into his possession. He tries to. So convinced am I of the correctness of my theory, so sure am I that that woman who has been found beneath the Lambeth arch is Jane Clinch, that, on my way to you, I sent a telegram to Scotland Yard, requesting them to send a detective at once."

"The deuce you have!" I stared at him. "I say, Pugh, it strikes me you are on the high road towards making of yourself a first-rate laughing stock. That new purchase of yours is going to make a fool of you."

Pugh was flying here and there about the room. I watched him with amazement—and amusement. He seemed half beside himself with excitement; he certainly is the most excitable man I have the pleasure of knowing. The truth is, his brain—such as it is—is saturated with nonsense: any cock-and-bull story is sufficient to set him running amok. I have known him hunt a ghost till it landed him in the mire of ignominious contumely. He believes in ghosts.

"You are wrong, Tress, you are wrong—I am sure of it. A clue has been placed in my hands towards the unmasking of a crime, and of a criminal, which I dare not neglect to follow. I sat up till two o'clock this morning listening to that woman's voice. Every repetition of it struck deeper horror. It was with me all night in dreams. I hear it now, speaking to me from every side. I feel that Providence has chosen me out to be an instrument of vengeance. I must not refuse to perform the office which has been thrust upon me."

"If I had sat up listening to that woman's voice till two o'clock this morning it would have haunted me in my dreams, unless I had drowned it in a bottle of brandy, which, under the circumstances, I probably should have done. If you take my advice, you will send that phonograph round to me for a day or two. By then the voice will have become less audible."

Pugh went and leaned his elbow on the corner of my mantelshelf. He made an effort to regain his self-control. He spoke more calmly:—

"I might have known that you would laugh at me; you always do. To you nothing is sacred—neither death nor the grave. Still, I venture to ask from you a favour. I confess that my nervous system is unstrung. I want you to come and be a witness of the interview which I am presently to have with the detective."

I hesitated, then consented. After all, the man, practically insane though he occasionally is, is the acquaintance of a lifetime.

"I'll come, on condition that in so doing I assume no sort of responsibility. I'm not going to have that detective of yours imagine that I had anything to do with sending for him, so don't you think it. I have a character for sanity to preserve."

"Come," he said, and he sighed.

We went. Pugh ventured on a prophecy as we got into the cab:—

"We shall find that detective waiting for us when we reach home."

He was wrong; we found nothing of the kind. What we did find was Pugh's man, Nalder, arguing with a fellow at the hall door, who seemed to be doing something to upset his—Nalder's—equilibrium. As the cab drove up, unless I am mistaken, the fellow was preventing the closing of the door by the simple and time-honoured process of thrusting his foot inside.

"Who is this?" asked Pugh as he bustled up the steps.

Both Nalder and the man with whom he was arguing seemed to be taken somewhat aback by the sudden appearance on the scene of the master of the house. Nalder endeavoured to explain.

"This man, sir, says he wishes to see you. He wouldn't believe me when I told him that you weren't at home."

Pugh turned towards the importunate visitor. He was a shabby, under-sized fellow with vagabond writ large all over him. He had on an ancient top hat and an ancient frock-coat, which was buttoned up just high enough in front to permit of a glimpse of an ancient paper collar. His face would have been improved by both shaving and washing, and he was in that condition which, in certain circles of society, would probably be described as having "had a drop." Pugh looked at him askance.

"Well, sir, what is it you want with me?"

The man put his hand up to his throat as if to settle in its place a wholly imaginary cravat.

"Is your name Pugh?"

Pugh owned that it was.

"I've come about my phonograph."

"About your——?"

Pugh paused, and stared, first at the speaker and then at me. He gave a step backwards. I could see that he was all in a fluster.

"Are you the man who sold the phonograph to the pawnbroker in the Fulham Road?"

"I am. And now he tells me you've got it. So I've come straight away to you. It's my living, and I want it back again, so that's all about it."

The man's manner did not seem to be much more prepossessing than his appearance. He struck me as spoiling for a fight. Pugh eyed him severely.

"Go into the house, sir. I will speak to you inside."

Apparently nothing loth, the man went into the house. As he went, Pugh, turning, spoke to me in a whisper:—

"The villain has delivered himself into our hands. On their arrival, the police will find their prisoner waiting."

The rapidity with which Pugh jumped at his conclusions and formed his plans took me aback. I remonstrated:—

"Don't you think you move a trifle quickly? You conjure up visions of actions for libels, and for false imprisonment, and similar amusing episodes."

For reply Pugh gripped my arm with uncomfortable violence.

"I tell you he has delivered himself into our hands—doesn't he look capable of any scoundrelism?"

I did not see the "sequitur." A man's capacity need have nothing to do with his performance.

But I did not wish to discuss the man upon the steps, while the man himself was watching us from inside the open door. Pugh led the way into a room, on a table in which still stood the phonograph. The stranger marched straight to it, displaying no inconsiderable impertinence.

"There is my phonograph."

Pugh laid his upon the article in question.

"This phonograph, sir, is mine!"

"Yours! How do you make that out? I bought it with my own money. It's my living. It was only because I had been having a drop that I sold it; I didn't get anything like its value. And now I want it back again. And I'm going to have it back again—so don't let there be any mistake."

Pugh looked the impudent individual in the face.

"You have been drinking, sir."

For this plain statement of a simple fact the stranger seemed to be unprepared. He looked about him askance. But he brazened it out:—

"You'd have been drinking if you had to go through what I have. I don't live in palaces."

The man waved his hat about him as if he intended his remark to have a personal application to the place in which Pugh himself resided.

"No, sir, you are more likely to be the occupant of a prison."

"Prison!" The man gave a startled glance over his shoulder. "Who's talking about a prison? I tell you what I'll do; I'll have a deal with you. I got two pound ten for this phonograph—as I tell you, I'd been drinking, and I never thought of pawning it, which I might have done, if I'd gone in by the other door. Two pound ten is every penny I got for it. You give me back the phonograph, and I'll give you back the two pound ten, in weekly instalments of half a crown."

The proposal was a cool one, to say the least of it. It did not seem to occur to the fellow that Pugh himself might have had to pay considerably more than two pound ten. But Pugh let that branch of the subject slide. He had something else upon his mind.

"Do you think that I don't know why you wish to get this phonograph back into your own possession?"

The man seemed to think the question an unnecessary one.

"It's my living; don't I tell you so?"

Pugh rested both his hands upon the phonograph; he leaned over it towards the stranger; he addressed him in a sepulchral whisper:—

"Yes, you do tell me that; but you do not tell me that if you don't get it back into your possession it may be your death."

The man laughed uneasily.

"If it isn't my living, I shouldn't be surprised if it was my death."

"You dare to tell me that, and to laugh at it?" The man seemed to be startled by Pugh's vehemence. "Do you think that this phonograph has not confided to me its secret?"

The man stared at Pugh, as if in amaze.

"Eh?"

"Your wife has spoken to me from out of this box."

Pugh brought his fist down with a bang upon the box which he alluded to.

"Go on! What are you talking about?"

Pugh accentuated his words by a sort of repetition: "Your poor ill-used wife."

The stranger seemed to be getting genuinely uneasy. He looked about him, from side to side, as if meditating a retreat. Pugh was evidently not according him the sort of reception he had looked forward to.

"I don't know that she got all the ill-usage—there were faults on both sides. Anyhow, I don't know what it's got to do with you. I've not come here to talk to you about my family matters, I've come about my phonograph."

"Driven by the haunting fear that it might tell all it knows!"

"Driven by what?"

"Driven by the memory of your wife's wild shrieks, lest the phonograph, the only witness of your ruffianism, should betray you, after all."

The fellow was getting into a very curious state of agitation. Pugh's melodramatic words and manner were undoubtedly impressive in their way, he really was so very much in earnest. They seemed to be affecting his visitor in a fashion which I, for one, had certainly not expected. A hunted look was coming on to his face and into his eyes.

"I don't know what you are talking about, and I don't want to know. I've come for my phonograph. You give it me back, and, as I say, I'll give you back the two pound ten in weekly installments of half a crown, I give you my word I will."

"You are too late. The phonograph already has betrayed you."

"Betrayed me! What do you mean?"

Pugh spoke in a whisper; in moments of excitement he is rather fond of whispering.

"What did you do to your wife?"

The stranger replied rather in a gasp, and then in a whisper:—

"My wife!"

"Yes, what did you do to your wife—your poor wife?"

"Nothing. I hardly touched her."

"You hardly touched her? You dare to tell me that, in the presence of the phonograph."

The stranger broke into a torrent of bad language, and into something else as well.

"I don't know what you're talking about. I tell you, I hardly touched her. It was her fault, she started me off. She ought to have left me alone, she knew I'd had a drop. When she liked, she'd drive a man stark raving mad; that's what she drove me, stark raving mad I was. I didn't know what I was doing. Then, when she wouldn't let me alone, I hit her—yes, I don't mind owning it, I hit her. I gave her what for. I'd do it again if I had a chance.

I'm a man, ain't I? Do you think I'm going to have my life made a hell on earth? Do you think I'm a slave, to be talked to, and ordered about by any woman that ever lived? No, not me: that's not the sort of man I am. I'd sooner hang for her any day of the week—that's me. Yes, and I'll hang for her to-morrow, willingly. And now you've got it—so there you are, and you can put it into your pipe and smoke it!"

The fellow wound up with another flood of imprecations. The violence of his manner was equal to the violence of his language. He flung his arms about, shook his head, stamped his feet, and generally "went on awful"! I do not know whether he surprised or tickled me most. He struck me as being, in his way, a character—one who, when he was, as he phrased it, stark raving mad, might be expected to make himself peculiarly objectionable.

Pugh listened to his outpourings with an air of unmitigated triumph. When he had finished he drew himself up with an "I-told-you-so" gesture and turned to me.

"Did I not tell you that Providence had chosen me out to be an instrument of vengeance? You have heard the scoundrel's confession issuing from between his crime-stained lips?"

"Don't you call me a scoundrel or I'll knock your flowery head off! Are you going to give me my phonograph or am I to take it?"

The scoundrel alluded to made a threatening movement in the direction of Pugh. Pugh modestly retreated.

"Take care how far you go, my man; we are not helpless women. I knew all that you have told us before you opened your mouth; unconsciously, you have but corroborated the evidence of the phonograph."

"The evidence of the phonograph?"

The man glared at Pugh, then at the phonograph, then back again at Pugh.

"As I have already told you, your fears were justified; the phonograph has revealed your guilt. Your name is Clinch?"

"What's my name got to do with you? You mind your own business; you take my tip, and do it!"

"You need not think to frighten us. I repeat, we are not helpless women. Your assumption of anger betrays you. I see your name is Clinch. Here, Mr. Clinch, are your poor wife's dying words."

Pugh handed him the sheet of paper on which he had written down the words which were uttered by the woman's voice as it proceeded from the phonograph. The fellow made no attempt to take the paper; but his jaw dropped open. I never saw a more remarkable change take place in a human countenance than took place in his. For the moment his tongue seemed partially paralysed.

"My wife's—last dying words! You don't mean—she's dead?"

"None should know better than you that I do mean that she is dead, since it was you who did her to death, since her innocent blood stains your murderous hands!"

"My God!"

"You cowardly villain!"

Pugh moved towards him. I thought for an instant he was going to strike him. The fellow would have suffered it; all the bluster had gone out of him. He had passed from a state of storm and fury to a state of collapse. He was trembling as with palsy. He seemed to be, all at once, in a condition of semi-stupefaction.

"I never meant to do it: I didn't know I'd done it; I only meant to give her a doing. I never—" the fellow hesitated; he gave a dreadful glance round the room—"I never stopped to see."

"You were mad drunk?"

"I was—I swear I was!"

"You were not conscious of what it was you did?"

"I wasn't—I swear I wasn't!"

"And while you were in that state, you attacked your helpless, unoffending wife, and you killed her, and you crammed her poor body into an egg-box, and, for all I know, alone and unassisted, in the dead of night, you conveyed that egg-box with its awful contents to what you hoped would be a secure hiding-place. But you were wrong—such a hope could only have been born of a drunkard's madness. The mutilated body of your murdered wife has been found."

"No, no, no! Gentlemen! gentlemen!" The fellow actually dropped on to his knees. "I never meant to do it—I swear I didn't! I didn't know what I was doing—I was mad drunk! If I'd been sober I wouldn't have touched her; I'd as soon have thought of hurting her as I would of hurting myself. Oh, Jane! You know I never meant to murder you!"

He raised his hands above his head in an agony of supplication. His abject self-abandonment was not a pleasant thing to contemplate. So even Pugh appeared to think.

"Get up, sir! It is not what you meant to do, it is what you did do which is the question. It is not us you must entreat, your entreaties must be directed elsewhere. Get up, I say!"

The man got up; directly he gained his feet he began backing towards the door. "Let me go! let me go!" he murmured.

But Pugh had no intention of doing anything of the kind. He moved quickly after him. "You will not be allowed to leave this room, my man, so you need not attempt it. Tress, see to the door."

I believe that, acting on Pugh's suggestion, I did interpose myself between the man and the door. The fellow looked at me, then at Pugh. He perceived that he was in a minority of one. His tone became a whine:—

"What are you going to do with me?"

"We are going to do the only thing which, as honest men, we can do—our duty. We are going to give you into the charge of the police."

"The police!" The words were rather screamed than spoken. "Don't do that—for God's sake, don't! Don't give me to the police. Have mercy! have mercy! I never meant to do it—don't I tell you that I swear I never meant to do it?"

Pugh was unbendingly stern.

"It is of no use for you to tell us anything. We have heard enough, and more than enough. I communicated with the police before you came; an officer of the law is already on the way. Whatever else you may have to tell must be told to him."

The fellow burst into another frenzy. He showered imprecations about him broadcast; he yelled and raved; he even wept; he cursed and entreated, threatened and implored. He behaved, in short, like a man bereft of his senses, working himself by degrees into a state of something very like delirium. From one point of view, it was a warm few minutes. It occurred to me that, with his drink-sodden brain, he had only to go a very little farther to become a dangerous madman. Every moment, indeed, I expected him to proceed from words to deeds. If he had, we should have found him a difficult customer to tackle. For my part, rather than engage in a hand-to-hand encounter with a homicidal lunatic, I should have preferred to let him go. His anxiety that we should allow him to adopt that course was unmistakable.

"Curse you! Let me go—let me go!"

He shrieked the words over and over again, advancing closer and closer towards me, with a dangerous something in his eyes, which looked to me as if he meant business at last. I was wondering whether, so far as I was personally concerned, it would not be advisable for me to grant his reiterated request, when, just before I had made up my mind, the door behind me opened, and an individual in a tweed suit was ushered in by Nalder.

The new comer introduced himself.

"I am a detective officer of police. I have come with reference to a telegram which was sent to Scotland Yard by a Mr. Pugh."

I do not think I was ever more glad to see a man in my life. I fancy, too, that the arrival of the representative of law and order relieved Pugh of a growing weight of anxiety.

"My name is Pugh; it was I who sent the telegram. You have arrived, officer, in the very nick of time. I give that man into custody on a charge of murder."

Pugh pointed to the wretched drunkard, who had subsided into shivering silence the moment the detective had appeared—as if he knew him. He shrank away, quivering like some frightened cur. The detective looked at Pugh, then at the miserable object in front of him; he seemed not quite to understand the situation.

"You give him into custody, you say, on a charge of murder; who has he murdered?"

"His wife. His name is Clinch. The body of his wife, Jane Clinch, was found yesterday, in an egg-box, under an arch in Lambeth. The man has confessed his guilt, in my friend's presence and my own. Here, besides, is a copy of his unfortunate wife's last dying words, in which she accuses him of killing her. They came into my possession in a way which may be described as almost miraculous. Indeed, if you will allow me to explain, you will perceive that the whole case is one of a most extraordinary character."

Pugh held out the record of the voice of the phonograph. The detective looked at it askance. He went a step forward, though whether it was towards the paper which Pugh was holding out to him, or whether it was towards the man, was more than I was clear about. The man, however, seemed to have no doubt upon the point. Directly the detective moved, without any sort of warning, he sprang at him like some wild animal, and, although the bigger man of the two, the officer, taken unawares, was borne backwards to the floor. Pugh, regardless of his spectacles, rushed to his assistance. In an amazingly short space of time, as nice a rough-and-tumble was taking place in Pugh's front-room as one would care to see. Since I had come into the house on the distinct understanding that I was to assume no sort of responsibility, I stood neutral. Not feeling that I was personally concerned in the proceedings, I permitted them to discuss the matter, in their own fashion, among themselves.

The two proved more than a match for the one. Presently the officer was standing up, holding his prisoner with a hand on either arm. He favoured him with a word or two of advice.

"Let's have no more of this. You'd better come quietly, or you'll be sorry."

The man looked sorry enough already. All the life seemed to have gone out of him, he seemed as limp as a rag. The detective took something from his jacket pocket. There was the gleam of metal. As he was about to adjust the handcuffs on the prisoner's wrists, I became conscious that a disturbance was taking place outside the door—a disturbance which was drawing rapidly nearer. Suddenly the door was flung wide open. A woman entered, by no means quietly, followed by the expostulating Nalder.

Nalder addressed himself to Pugh, apologetically:

"I told her not to come upstairs, sir, but she would come."

"Of course I would; what do you think?" retorted the woman, not exactly *sotto voce.*

She was a short, slight woman, covered almost from head to foot by an old cloth jacket. The ruins of a bonnet were on her head. It was almost impossible to make out her features, owing to the fact that bandages concealed almost the whole of her head and face. Only one eye was left uncovered, but that was sufficient to enable her to perceive the man whom the detective was just about to handcuff.

"Jack!" she cried.

At the sound of the woman's voice, another surprising change took place in Mr. Clinch's bearing. He twisted himself, like an eel, out of the policeman's grasp, and rushed between her outstretched arms.

"Jane!" he cried. "My God, old girl, I'm glad to see you! They told me you was dead!"

"Dead!—me dead? I look as if I was dead, don't I?"

"They said I'd killed you!"

"You killed me? Go on!"

"They did—straight, they did! And they said I'd packed your body into an egg-box, and it had been found, and you'd given me away. I thought I must have done it when I was howling drunk, and I was in a state, old girl! and they gave me into charge for murdering you."

"They gave you into charge for murdering me! Well! the likes of that! Never mind old man"—the fellow was blubbering like a booby on the woman's shoulder—"you're all right. They won't touch you. You haven't done no harm, as we'll soon show 'em."

"Who's this woman?" inquired the detective. He seemed to be a little dazed.

"Who are you calling a woman? I'm his wife, that's who I am, and he's my husband—what do you want with my husband?"

The detective turned to Pugh, in not unnatural bewilderment.

"Is this woman his wife? I thought you said that you gave the man into charge for the murder of his wife."

In his efforts at assisting the detective to secure Mr. Clinch, Pugh had had his spectacles broken. Without them he was as blind as a bat. He was peering about him for another pair.

"Exactly. His poor wife is dead. There is unimpeachable evidence to prove it. This woman must be an impostor."

The woman went striding across the room towards Pugh, righteous indignation in her voice and in her bearing.

"Who are you calling an impostor? You take care who you're calling names, or I'll know the reason why. I'm his lawful married wife, that's who I am. My name's Jane Clinch, and I've got my marriage lines in my pocket. His name's John Clinch, and I was married to him in Chelsea Parish Church four years ago come the thirteenth day of May. There you are— look at that! That's my certificate of marriage!"

She flourished a very much folded sheet of paper under Pugh's nose. Pugh looked at her, as best he could without his glasses, as if he could not make her out at all.

"But, my good woman, the man has just now confessed to having murdered his wife, in my own presence."

The man in question promptly denied the soft impeachment.

"I didn't do anything of the kind—that's where you're wrong, and that's where you've been wrong all through. I told you I'd been giving her a doing, as I had—you can take and have a look at her if you doubt me— more shame to me. Mind, though I wouldn't have touched her if I hadn't been having a drop; but it was you who said I'd murdered her, and stuffed her body into an egg-box, and I don't know what."

"So he had been giving me a doing," corroborated the lady. "That's all right enough! And if a man can't lay his hands on his own lawful married wife, I should like to know who can?" She turned to her husband. "But it wasn't nice of you, Jack, to go and leave me all this time; how was I to know what had become of you? They told me at 'The Bricklayer's Arms' that you'd sold the phonograph at Barton's, in the Fulham Road. I went to Barton's, and I saw you just coming out, so I followed you here. Then I saw the bobby come—I know a copper when I see one, I do hope!"—this with a contemptuous glance at the detective in his tweeds, "so, I says, I wonder what's up now? So I thought I'd come in and see for myself, and it seems to me that it's lucky for you I did come."

"It was lucky," murmured Mr. Clinch, "I own it was."

Pugh still seemed unable to grasp the actualities of the situation; I fancy, too, he was unwilling to grasp them, the attitude of his mind had been so decisive on the subject of that phonographic tragedy. He had found another pair of glasses: through them he had glanced at me. He had seen that I was smiling; I do not think he liked it.

He made a final attempt to prove that murder had been done.

"If, as you say, your name is Jane Clinch, what explanation have you to give of this. You will find, woman, that, to satisfy me, your explanation will have to be of the fullest and most comprehensive kind; no subterfuge, however plausible it may seem, will do."

He held out the record of the voice of the phonograph, with, as he did so, a sidelong glare towards me. Directly she perceived, with her one eye, what was written on the paper, the lady laughed.

"Well, I never! if he hasn't written down my record! You remember, Jack, my mentioning to you that the people about King's Road seemed to have got a bit tired of military bands and comic songs, and such like, and as how I thought it might be good business if we was to give 'em a bit of real life—something as would curdle 'em?"

"I remember it quite well," Mr. Clinch acknowledged. "It was only last week you said it."

"Last Wednesday it was, the night before you gave me a doing. And do you remember how I sat down then and there, and how you laughed at me when I made a new record into the receiver, with your helping me, pretending as how you was a-murdering me, and all the rest of it; and do you remember as how I told you to label it 'A Drama in Real Life,' and stick the name upon the notice-board along with the others, and see if it didn't fetch the pennies from the gals as liked to shiver? Well, dashed if the old josser hasn't took the record down on paper, screams and all! Straight, he has!"

CHAPTER III

THE PENNYWORTH

Pugh handed back the phonograph to Mr. Clinch, free, gratis, and for nothing. Although it had been for so short a time in his possession, he had had quite enough of it—indeed, he had had too much. He made no allusion to the return of that two pound ten, even in weekly instalments of half a crown. He not only made Mr. Clinch a present of his former property, but he gave him a five-pound note as well, and something to his wife, and something to the detective, too. In fact, just then, I believe, he would have given something to any one who had chosen to ask for it. He felt very sore, poor Pugh!

He does not seem to have cared much for phonographs since. His interest in their development seems to have died away. I have noticed that, whenever any allusion is made to them in his presence, he always seems to bridle, and, if possible, to change the theme. He has explained to me, on more than one occasion, with every appearance of gravity, that he cannot understand how he ever came to make such an ass of himself. He does talk like that, when he has been making an idiot of himself in a fresh direction. And then he repeats the performance on the very smallest provocation.

Not long since, I was walking along the King's Road, Chelsea, when, standing on a barrow in the gutter, I came upon a phonograph, which was intended to delight the public for the small sum of a penny a "go." It was in charge of Mr. and Mrs. Clinch. I recognised them at once, though they were both of them looking in better feather than when I first encountered them.

A board was suspended over the instrument, which informed you of the pleasant things which you could have for your penny. Number ten on the list was, "A Drama in Real Life." All the tubes were disengaged just then, and I had the affair all to myself. I paid my penny. I called for number ten; and I confess, when the woman's voice broke upon my ear, and I listened to the whole performance, I was startled again. I had had some acquaintance with phonographs since my introduction to them by Pugh; I certainly never had heard anything so realistic. It really was not strange, considering his peculiar mental calibre, and the circumstances under which he had first heard it, that that record had caused Pugh to make an exhibition of himself.

Mrs. Clinch must have been in a singular frame of mind, or body, or both, when she made it. After all, I cannot help thinking that that affection-ate husband of hers must have been giving her a "doing" at the time. The whole thing—those screams in particular—did sound so very much like earnest!

In its way, it was worth a penny to listen to—especially if one liked to be "curdled." I should not be surprised to learn that that particular record was very popular in the neighbourhood, though I should not have cared to pay for it quite so much as Pugh had done.

THE ADVENTURE OF THE CABINET

(MR. PUGH TELLS THE STORY)

CHAPTER I

THE CAPTURE

I could scarcely believe that it was Tress when I saw him coming down the little garden in front of the house. His most generous critic would scarcely say that the pure, virtuous air of the country was suited to him. He, on his part, seemed equally surprised to see me—as though I had not been a lover of the country from my youth!

"What are you doing here?" he demanded—as though I had been a trespasser upon his property.

"Rather, what are you doing here? I find in rural simplicity a sympathetic atmosphere. In straying beside the limpid waters, I find that refreshment which my soul most loves. But you, Tress—what attraction can Arcadian Sunbury have for such as you?"

"Pugh, I believe you're the greatest humbug that ever lived." He came out of the little garden, shutting the wicket gate behind him with a bang. He seemed quite angry. "Are you coming up to town?"

"Shortly, Tress, shortly. At present, I am about to cast a line into the shimmering stream."

"A line?—'A worm at one end and a fool at the other'—I know! Come along!"

"Gently, Tress, gently! Don't quite pull me off my legs. I am sorry that the punt which I have engaged does not contain a seat for you, but I never dreamt that you would ever come to Sunbury."

"Do you think that I would sit on a dirty wooden chair fishing for tittlebats at the rate of half a crown a fish?" He turned on me with a savage sneer. "Look here, Pugh, are you really going fishing?"

"Really, Tress, I don't know what affair of yours it is, but—I am."

"Well, you may comfort yourself with the reflection that those who were born to be hanged can never be drowned."

These were the farewell words which my dear old friend flung after me as he departed. There is not a more discourteous man in England than Joseph Tress. I say it, and, as I have known him pretty well my whole life long, I ought to know.

"I wonder," I asked myself, as he walked off, "what he is doing in Sunbury? He seldom goes to a place without having some definite end in view, and that an end, very often, which will not bear the light of day. I wonder what he was doing in that house which he came out of. He evidently did not like my seeing him come out of it. When he is gone, I will go and see what sort of house it is."

I waited till I was sure he had gone. And, for that purpose, I strolled down to the river-side, so that if he looked back, or retraced his steps, he might have no suspicion of a desire on my part to pry into his affairs. That man is himself so continually guilty of mean and even sordid actions, that he is in a chronic state of doubt as to the motives which actuate even his oldest friends.

I hung about the water's edge for, I daresay, half an hour, and then, as I knew a train left for London about that time, I took it for granted that he had gone by it, and that the coast was clear. So I strolled leisurely towards the house out of which I had seen him come.

It was an old-fashioned, rather dilapidated little house; the merest cottage, in fact. In one of the windows hang a bill: "This House and Furniture to be Sold. Inquire Within."

"Ah," I told myself, "that's what Mr. Tress is after. Now I understand!"

I knew that Joseph Tress would go any distance if he saw a chance of adding to the lot of trumpery which he calls his collection. I thought it probable that he had heard, in some surreptitious and underhand way, of some curio which was to be had for a song in this outlandish place, and had immediately come rushing after it. Joseph Tress is the sort of man who, if he supposed that the vendor was ignorant of the value of the thing which he was selling, would, with a clear conscience, offer him less than the hundredth part of what it was actually worth. But, if I could help it, I had no intention of allowing innocence to be imposed upon by him.

So I strolled up the garden and knocked at the cottage door.

The door was opened by a shrivelled-up, middle-aged woman in rusty black, who looked as if she were in a continual state of tearfulness; just the kind of unprotected female whom Joseph Tress would delight in imposing on.

"Has Mr. Tress been here?"

She sniffed. I should say, from her appearance, that she was a sort of woman who had sniffed from childhood.

"Yes, sir, a gentleman of that name has been here,—leastways, that's the name upon the card he gave me. He's not long been gone."

"Ah!" She did not invite me to enter. But I entered without an invitation. There was no hall. One passed from the garden straight into what seemed to be the sitting-room. "Mr. Tress came after the house and furniture?"

She sniffed again. This seemed to be the sort of woman one would like to have always within sight—and sound.

"Yes, sir, he did—leastways, he said he did."

"What are you asking?"

"Well, sir, for the house and furniture—the house is leasehold, there's twenty-two years to run, but, of course, the furniture's my own—what I asked Mr. Tress was three hundred and fifty pounds for everything."

The sum was not a large one, but it struck me that, to say the least of it, it was as much as the property was worth—I doubted if the cottage would hold together for two and twenty years. As for the furniture, if what I could see of it was an example of the rest, I would rather be without it, though it were offered to me as a gift.

She began a long rigmarole about how she'd kept house for her uncle, and he had died and left her the house and furniture, which was all very well in its way, but not of much use if you'd nothing else to keep body and soul together; so she thought she'd like to sell it and put the money into a business which a relation had in town—and so on, and so on, and I don't know what else besides. While she yarned we wandered from room to room, each one smaller and fustier than the other.

"I should say, sir, that the house and the furniture is as good as sold. Mr. Tress as good as said he would let me have the money in the morning."

The woman's sudden observation took me aback.

"Do you mean to tell me that Mr. Tress said that he would buy the place?"

I imagine that something in the tone of my voice caused the lady to slightly bridle.

"Well, sir, he said he would, and, of course, as I took him for a gentleman, I took him at his word."

I could but suppose that Tress had been having a jest at the unprotected female's expense. He is always ready, even in search of what he calls amusement, to take advantage of the helpless. It was absurd to suppose that anything about the place could have an attraction for him. I pictured to myself the saturnine smile which had been upon his face while he practised on the woman's credulity.

"This," she said, as we entered the last apartment the house contained, "is my uncle's bedroom. It was always kept for him. In it he was born, and in it he died."

Then in that case I felt that her uncle had my sympathy. A man who had been born, and who died, in a room like that, was deserving of any man's sympathy, even Tress'. It was a fair-sized room, but it smelt. It was badly lighted. There was only one small window. The ceiling was so low that you could touch it with your hand; while such furniture as it contained—I gave a sudden start. I made a dash at something which was standing between the bed and the wall.

"My uncle used to use that as a sort of desk," the woman commented as I made my dash. "He used to keep his papers in it, and that kind of thing. Mr. Tress, he noticed it particular. I have heard that it's worth money."

Worth money! I was trembling. I was speechless. I scarcely knew whether I was standing on my head or heels. What I was gazing at was a genuine Louis Quatorze cabinet; as fine an example of the period as the world contains. I saw it at a glance, and I say it without hesitation—I have seen with my own eyes a cabinet, no whit better than that, sold for nine thousand pounds. It had received scandalous ill-usage. That barbarian of an uncle had used it as a sort of desk! But I perceived in an instant that the damage done was merely superficial. A few touches from a skilful hand and it would be as good as ever. How the cabinet got there the Lord only knows, but there it was.

"So Mr. Tress noticed it, did he?"

I asked the question rather to gain time than for anything else. Trust Tress to notice it, if it was there to notice!

"Yes, sir, he did. And it was after he noticed it that he said he would buy the house."

No wonder! Now I understood the nefarious machinations of the double-minded Tress. I had to keep my face turned away, lest the woman should perceive my agitation. My mind was made up in a second. That man might take advantage of the ignorant innocence of an unprotected female, but he should not take advantage of me. Making a great effort to regain my self-control, I faced round to her.

"I will buy the house myself. It is just the sort of thing I want. I will give you my cheque for it at once."

She seemed astonished. I fancy that my previous depreciation of the place and all that it contained had been pretty obvious. So that my sudden offer took her by surprise.

"Your cheque?" She hesitated. "Well, sir, you see you're quite a stranger to me, and Mr. Tress as good—"

"Do you know Mr. ——?" I mentioned the landlord of a famous local hostelry.

"Know him!" She spoke of him with a sort of reverential awe.

"If I bring him here, and he assures you that my cheque is good for three hundred and fifty pounds will that content you?"

"Perfectly."

So I fetched that landlord then and there, and he assured her that if she liked he would exchange cheques with me, and she might have his cheque instead of mine. Then she hummed and hawed about having as good as sold the place to Tress. So I offered to give her another twenty pounds if she would give me immediate possession, and would, in fact, clear off the premises at once. And the end of it was, that, for three hundred and seventy pounds, I bought the house and all it contained—including that Louis Quatorze cabinet. I took the cabinet up with me then and there to town. I was not going to experience, in my own case, a verification of the proverb about there being many a slip 'twixt cup and lip. I knew Tress so well! I knew that if by any chance he returned while that cabinet was still upon the premises, and found that I had prevented his imposing on the ignorant innocence of that aged and half-witted female, that he would be quite capable of taking possession of my property, even though, to enable him to do so, he had to resort to violence and highway robbery.

CHAPTER II

THE TRIUMPH OF POSSESSION

It was a magnificent example—magnificent! The more closely I regarded my new purchase, the more its excellence impressed itself upon me. There are cabinets, the productions of admitted masters, which in some important requisite fall short of even a moderate standard. Just as a great painter does not always produce great paintings, so the great cabinetmakers were sometimes false to their own greatness. Every connoisseur can put his finger upon an undoubted illustration. But this cabinet of mine was perfect—perfect! It needed slightly renovating. It had been shamefully ill-used. That old woman's old idiot of an uncle had actually spilt a pot of ink upon one of the shelves! But I felt persuaded that it needed nothing done to it which I myself was not capable of doing. I have not been a collector all these years without becoming master of a trick or two. I had had it placed in my drawing-room, where the light of the centre window could fall upon it. And I was telling myself that at last my almost lifelong researches had been adequately rewarded, and I had become the possessor of something which all the world would envy me, when—Joseph Tress came in!

Unannounced. He is not the sort of man to trouble himself about observing the ordinary decencies of civilised life. He stood at the door with his hat on, and, without even condescending to say good-morning, he shook his walking-stick at me, and said:—

"You thief!"

I am not the sort of man to allow myself to be trampled on even by a Joseph Tress. I let him see this by the manner in which I returned his gaze.

"Mr. Tress!" was all I condescended to observe.

So far from showing any signs of being impressed by the proper yet dignified air of resentment which I displayed, he forgot himself so far as actually to repeat the obnoxious epithet which he had already once applied to me. Then crossing the room, he stood in front of my newly-purchased cabinet.

"My beauty! My treasure!"

Stretching out his arms to it, he spoke in a tone of passionate emotion which, at any rate, was creditable to his knowledge and his taste.

"Yes, it is a beauty, is it not? I am glad, Tress, to find that even you can see that."

"A beauty?" He turned upon me with a degree of violence which would scarcely have been justifiable even if I had contradicted him. "By——! its the finest thing I ever saw!"

"Yes, I really think it is; the finest thing. It is certainly a genuine Boule."

"A genuine Boule!" He touched it with the finger-tips of his right hand, as a lover might touch the soft cheek of his mistress. "It's the finest thing Boule ever did. Have you ever seen such chasing?"

"No; I don't think I ever have."

"And such scroll-work?"

"It is superb, Tress, superb!"

"The whole design, both in conception and in execution, is just perfect. As I live, there's not such another cabinet in all the world. Talk about that Hamilton thing! I don't mean to say that that is not worth the twelve thousand pounds which was paid for it—but it's not to be named in the same breath with this."

"It is a truly magnificent work of art—truly magnificent! I feel that myself. It pleases me, Tress, to find myself in agreement with you, for once in a way, on such a matter as this. Indeed, I will go so far as to ask you to allow me to congratulate you on your good taste."

I held out my hand to him, with what, I trust, was a sufficiently Christian-like obliviousness of the man's notoriously bad character.

"Agreement with you?" He turned to me with a smile upon his face which I did not like. He put his hand behind his back. "May I ask, Mr. Pugh, how it is that I find my cabinet in your drawing-room?"

"Your cabinet? Pray, Mr. Tress, what do you mean?"

"Are you aware, Mr. Pugh, that men have been sentenced to penal servitude for life for less offences than that of which you have apparently been guilty?"

"I trust, Mr. Tress, that, when you have made yourself quite plain, it may not become necessary for me to have to ring for Nalder to conduct you to the door."

He paused before he ventured to continue his insolent suggestions. He eyed me with what, considering the man's own moral standard, I am proud to say were not glances of respect and admiration. He stretched out his arm, so suddenly and so far, that he almost thrust his finger in my face.

"When I met you yesterday, at Sunbury, I was conscious of a sudden impulse which suggested that I should pick you up, and put you in the water, and hold you there till you were drowned. What a service I should have rendered to humanity had I acted on what was evidently an inspiration from on high."

"My good Mr. Tress, all the world is so well acquainted with the fashion in which you, unfortunately, allow yourself to talk, that, I can assure you, nothing which you may please to say will have any effect on me whatever."

"That, Mr. Pugh, I entirely believe. I believe that nothing which any honest man could say to you would have any effect on you whatever. You are an illustration of the truth that an individual can sink to such a state of degradation as that. So you watched me out of sight, and, directly my back was turned, robbed the old lady."

"On the contrary, I saved her from being robbed by you."

"I see. That is how you put it. Ingenious ingenuous, Mr. Pugh! You are not aware that I had already purchased the cabinet; that is, that I had already robbed the old lady, before you, the second and the greater robber, appeared upon the scene?"

"I am aware that you had done nothing of the kind."

"No? You are at least aware that I had told the old lady that I would purchase the cabinet—that is, that I would rob her—and that I had merely gone up to town in search of the funds with which to consummate my evil deed. Your presence of mind was greater than mine. I was so overwhelmed with joy at discovering so easy a method of committing a great dishonesty that it never occurred to me that, in that doghole of a place, I, a stranger, could palm off my unsupported cheque for three hundred and fifty pounds, even upon such a vestige of primeval innocence as that old lady."

"I know nothing, and I wish to know nothing, either of your movements or of your intentions, Mr. Tress. And, as this is a sort of discussion in which I take no interest, and which I, indeed, particularly dislike, I must request you, with all possible civility, to allow me to say good-day."

"Good-day? So this is your idea of a good-day, is it, Mr. Pugh? Well, we shall see. Before I do say good-day, I wish to clearly understand if you can have any intention of continuing in the possession of my property, Mr. Pugh?"

I rubbed the palms of my hands together. I perceived his discomfiture; I pitied him.

"My good Mr. Tress, you may clearly understand that I have every intention of continuing in the perpetual possession of the inimitable treasure which my good fortune has enabled me to purchase."

"You understand that you came into possession of it by means of a trick—a mean and a dirty trick. That you have not only robbed an old woman, but that you have also robbed your oldest friend."

"My funny Mr. Tress, you should make some attempt to conceal your chagrin, you really should. But it is a fine thing, is it not? Possibly the finest example extant of the famous M. Boule!"

"As you say, it is possibly the finest example extant of the famous M. Boule. Just as you are, possibly, the finest example extant of—another kind of thing! Now, Mr. Pugh, I have the pleasure of wishing you good-day."

Without any further ceremony he left the room; he had never removed his hat during the whole of the interview. He played the boor—none could better play the part—to the end. As he went down the stairs I stood at the top and called out to Nalder to open the door for Mr. Tress. As I did so Tress stood still. He called out at the top of his voice:—

"If any male animal who is content to have a thief for a master dares to attempt to lackey me, I'll break my stick across his head."

"In that case," I observed, "do not trouble, Nalder."

Nalder did not trouble. Joseph Tress let himself out of the house with a bang.

CHAPTER III

THE ANGUISH OF THE PARTING

Nearly a month went by. I revelled—without exaggeration I may use the word; who would not have revelled?—in the possession of my glorious cabinet. Every day I discovered in it new beauties. Surely never was there a happier man than I. I was beginning to hope that I was finally rid of Joseph Tress. That after his egregious and scandalous misbehaviour on the occasion of our last encounter, that even he would not have sufficient assurance ever again to attempt to thrust himself under my notice. But, in so hoping, I was reckoning without my host. I was soon to learn that there was noth-ing—nothing! of which such a creature was not capable.

I had renovated the cabinet. I had done it all myself. I had found, as I expected, that I required no extraneous assistance—professional renovators, with any pretence to skill, are such robbers! Once more the cabinet stood revealed, every whit as spick and span, and as glorious as when it had received its creator's final touches. One morning I was gazing at it with the sense of reverential awe which is only found in the true connoisseur whose soul is attuned to higher things, when again—Joseph Tress came in.

Always unannounced! Had he been announced I should certainly have refused the man admission. This time as he entered, he did have the decency to remove his hat. He crossed the room with an air of confident familiarity, as though I had parted from him on the best of terms only an hour ago. He confronted the cabinet.

"So, Pugh, you have it still?"

"Yes, Mr. Tress, I have it still. I don't know if you imagined that I had given it away since I had the pleasure of seeing you last."

"Given it away? Hardly, Pugh—not you! I perceive you have been doing it up. Your hand betrays itself. You don't do that sort of thing badly for an amateur, but it is a pity that you could not find it in your—heart to spare a five pound for a competent workman, Pugh!"

It was only the fellow's insolence—I let it pass. Indeed, I was so annoyed at the man's presumptuous intrusion that I hardly knew how to evince my just resentment, without at the same time doing violence to my sense of dignified decorum. He went on, outwardly indifferent, as became a person of his pachydermatous constitution, to the scorn with which I eyed him.

"But even a workman of your limited capacity has been able to make it look a little better than it did before. It is a wonderful thing—wonderful, indeed! By the way, wasn't Finch the name of the old woman from whom you bought it?"

"May I ask, Mr. Tress, why you inquire?"

"Oh, nothing—nothing! I never saw anything like the engraving of these centre figures! It resembles the perfect workmanship of which one only dreams. Wasn't Fir Cottage the name of the place in which she lived?"

"Again, Mr. Tress, may I ask why you inquire?"

"Well, I don't mind telling you, not in the least. There's an advertisement in a paper which I have in my pocket, which I think may be of interest to you."

He laid his hat and stick upon the chair. He took a newspaper from his pocket. Placing his glasses in position on his nose he unfolded the paper.

"Perhaps you might like me to read it aloud to you—this is the advertisement to which I refer:—

"'One thousand two hundred and fifty pounds reward.—Whereas a cabinet, a Boule Armoire, a unique example of the master, of the estimated value of ten thousand pounds, was confided, for safe keeping, to Mrs. Finch, at that time of Fir Cottage, Sunbury; and, since Mrs. Finch has disappeared from that address, there is reason to believe that she has disposed of the cabinet. This is to give notice that a Reward of Two Hundred and Fifty Pounds will be paid for such information as shall lead to the apprehension and conviction of the purchaser; and that a further Reward of One Thousand Pounds will be given for such information as shall lead to the recovery of the stolen property. Information to be given to Messrs. Delebat, Dibbs & Gale, 37 Lincoln's Inn Fields, or at any Police Station.'

"There, Pugh, perhaps you would like to read the advertisement for yourself? I daresay you might find it rather interesting reading."

Smoothing out the paper, Tress laid it on the table by which I was standing. I was conscious, all of a sudden, of one of those attacks of palpitation of the heart, to which I have been subject from my early youth, and which, when they visit me, always make me feel as though I suffered from weakness of the knees. I was aware that Tress was regarding me with a hideous distortion of countenance, which he probably intended for a grin.

"What's the matter, Pugh? You don't look well."

"It's a passing indisposition, Mr. Tress. I—have always been subject to these qualms."

"Indeed? That's sad! Especially as I should imagine that you will shortly suffer from sufficient qualms, apart from any which may come to you as a mere result of constitution."

I sat down. I read the advertisement with difficulty. My eyes, all at once, had grown so dim, that my spectacles were scarcely of any assistance. By the time I had got to the end of it the room seemed to be whirling round and round.

"Good heavens, Tress, what an awful thing!"

"How so? Your prescience was not at fault. As you hinted, on the occasion of our last pleasant little interview, you saved me from committing robbery by becoming yourself the thief."

"Tress, what shall I do?"

"What shall you do? I don't think, my dear Pugh, that the question is, what will you do? I think that the question is, rather, what will be done to you? I have always understood that if the receiver of the missing Gainsborough were ever discovered that he would get penal servitude for life. I imagine that this case will be found on all fours with that. I should say that you will get penal servitude for life—for the remainder of your life, that is."

"Tress, don't—don't talk nonsense!"

"Nonsense! You call penal servitude for life, nonsense? Well, men's notions differ. I shouldn't call penal servitude for life nonsense—but, as I say, each man has his own ideas. At any rate, it will be twelve hundred and fifty pounds in my pocket."

"Twelve hundred and fifty pounds in your pocket, Tress! What do you mean?"

"Haven't you read the advertisement? Am not I in a position to give information which will lead to the apprehension and conviction of the purchaser, and to the recovery of the stolen property, too?"

"Tress, is it conceivable that you can for a moment contemplate the possibility of consigning, with your own hand, the friend of your boyhood's days, of your early manhood, of your riper years, to what may prove to be the horrors of a living tomb?"

"My dear Pugh, no melodrama, if you please. Some one is sure to claim the reward, and why shouldn't it be me? Why should I put twelve hundred and fifty pounds into some one else's pockets? If, as you say, I am your life-long friend, you yourself should be glad to be able to do a good turn to your friend, rather than to a perfect stranger, on the occasion of what may turn out to be your final disappearance from the world."

"Tress, I don't know if you are jesting. I prefer to believe that you are—"

"Play the man, Pugh—play the man! I have strained a point to come and give you information of the advertisement's having appeared. If you like you can rob me of two hundred and fifty pounds by making a bolt of it before I can set the police upon your track, but the thousand for the recovery of the stolen property I mean to have."

"Tress—"

"On my honour, Pugh, you sicken me. You have the courage to conceive a gigantic robbery—because you were as well aware that it was a robbery as I was—"

"On my word of honour, Tress, I had no notion—"

"Don't lie to me, sir,—not to me. We're a couple of thieves. I knew that it was a robbery, and you knew that it was a robbery, only you happened to land the plunder first. And now that detection, and, of course, punishment stares you in the face, you stand there quivering and shivering like a well-whipped mongrel rather than a clean-bred man."

"Is it possible that I have endeavoured all my life to live as becomes an honest, and a Christian gentleman—"

"Stuff, Pugh, stuff! Pitch that yarn to the judge from the dock, if you like, but not to me."

"Tress, old friend—"

"Stand back, sir! Don't paw me about! Don't soil me with the touch of a coward and a thief! Hang me if I'm not worth a dozen such men as you. To prove it—I'll tell you what I'll do—I'll take your guilt upon my shoulders."

"You'll take my guilt upon your shoulders? Tress, you are so violent. You know how I suffer from a nervous affection. You bewilder me. Tell me, clearly and quietly, what it is you mean."

"You old—fox! I'll tell you clearly enough, if not quietly enough, as well. I'll give you the three hundred and fifty pounds which you gave to that old hag, and I'll be the purchaser of the cabinet instead of you. Do you think I should fear penal servitude for life if it were mine? By —— Pugh, I believe I would submit to being broken on the wheel, if I might be the owner of such a cabinet, by Boule."

His language was dreadful. His violence painful in the extreme. I had never had so clear a glimpse of the depths of depravity of which the man was capable. I flatter myself, not, I believe, without reason, that I am an enthusiastic collector. But his enthusiasm went farther than mine. Penal servitude for life, or anything like penal servitude for life, would, in my judgment, be too high a price to pay for all the treasures of art which the world contains. Before, and above all things, honesty, and the reputation of honesty for me. Still I was not disposed to allow Tress to find in me too pliable a subject.

"Suppose you were to give me the three hundred and fifty pounds as you suggest—three hundred and seventy pounds was really what I paid—and we share the cabinet between us. Have in it a sort of joint ownership, as it were."

"Joint ownership be hanged! You'll be suggesting next that it should remain in your possession."

"I certainly was thinking of suggesting something of the kind. You see, Tress, the cabinet is mine."

"You say so! Say so to the gentleman in blue who will call on you when I have paid my visit to Lincoln's Inn Fields. Listen to me, Pugh. Sell me the cabinet absolutely, now, at once! and let me take the consequences. Or—I have a cab at the door!—I go straight from this room to Lincoln's Inn Fields to lay the required information."

"My dear Tress, this is a matter—you yourself must perceive that this is a matter which requires reflection."

"Not an hour—not a moment, sir! Make up your mind upon the nail! Are you to go to jail, or I? That is the simple question which I propose for your solution."

I could not understand him. It seemed to me so incredible a thing that a man, calling himself a gentleman, could be willing, and seemingly, anxious, to sacrifice the liberty, and the happiness, and, it might be, the very existence, of the friend of a lifetime, in exchange for a sum of money, no matter how large that sum might be, that I found myself unable to realise that even a man like Joseph Tress could be capable of so great a villainy. But I was far from giving him credit for his whole capacity for crime!

I let him have the cabinet—my heart's best treasure! the thing of beauty which I loved almost as I loved my life. But as I read and read again that hideous advertisement, and as I became more and more conscious what manner of man this really was, and how his fingers itched for the blood-money which would come to him as the price of his friend, I felt that this was a matter in which, to say the least of it, my reputation might be at stake. No man was ever more conscious of innocence, no man was ever more keenly aware that his motives and his actions had alike been above suspicion. But I knew how simple honesty is apt to be misjudged by a too censorious world. And how constitutionally dishonest men, like Joseph Tress, are constrained, by stress of circumstances, to judge others by their own low standards.

He haggled about the price. I pointed out to him, as clearly as I could, how just it was that I should make some slight profit on the transaction. That I was, at any rate, entitled to some interest on my money, during the time I had been out of pocket. But it was with difficulty that I induced him to even return to me the three hundred and seventy pounds which I had originally paid. He more than hinted that I was swindling him out of twenty pounds, and that three hundred and fifty pounds was all that I had given.

"Now," said he, when I had extracted from him the final sovereign, "if you will let me have some canvas, and a cord, I'll cover it up, and take it away with me, outside the cab."

"My dear Tress, why such undue haste? I was at least hoping that you would allow me to spend a few hours with it in silent communion, so that in solitude I might bid it a long farewell. Indeed, I think that you might allow me to spend with it still another night."

He looked at me—though it would be more correct to say, he glared.

"Pugh, what do you take me for? If I were to allow you to spend even one hour with it, in what you call silent communion, I might bid it a long farewell. Before I returned, burglars would have appeared upon the scene, and the cabinet would have vanished from my eyes for ever, like a dream." And this was the man whom I had once esteemed my friend!

I found him some canvas and some cord. I am glad to say that I made him pay me five shillings for the two, which, at a moderate estimate, was some four or five times what they were worth. He covered the cabinet. I let him do it unassisted. I declined to lend a hand. Nor would I permit Nalder, or any of my servants, to have a finger in the pie. Through the window, he called the cabman up; a coarse, vulgar person, with whom he was immediately on terms of jovial familiarity. Between them they bore the cabinet down the stairs and through the hall, and I saw them place it on the cab. When the cab had vanished, and, with it my cabinet, I sat down at a table, and I covered my face with my hands, and, I am not ashamed to say, I wept. My cabinet! my cabinet! I have passed the meridian of life, I seldom shed a tear, and an outsider may be unable to see in such a situation as mine sufficient cause for the opening of the fountains of my grief. But such an one can be no genuine collector, and he can never have possessed a Boule Armoire.

CHAPTER IV

THE TRAITOR

How empty the room seemed now that it had gone! How its presence had glorified the chamber! I paced to and fro as I began to control the outward tokens of my sorrow. My heart burned with rage within my breast. False, false friend! That villain Tress, who, for a sum of money, would have betrayed his friend! Where had I put the paper in which was the advertisement? I glanced about the room. I started; it was gone! The scoundrel of a Tress, taking advantage of my agitation, had pocketed it when my back was turned, and taken it and the cabinet away with him together.

So! He thought that he had tricked me once again. He thought that he had fooled me to the top of my bent. Let him not make too sure of that. After all, I am not a man whom it is easy to trick. Even a worm, when it is trodden on, will sometimes turn. The man's cynical dishonesty revolted me! He knew what I had not known, that the cabinet was stolen, that it had never been the old woman's property to sell. Had I for a moment suspected that she proposed that I should play the part of receiver to her thief, I should have shrunk from her with horror, and with scorn. But this man Tress, having failed in robbing aged ignorance, had not only robbed his friend, but he had robbed the innocent stranger to whom the cabinet, in fact, belonged. What a catalogue of crime! As I began to picture to myself what, indeed, must be the feelings of the rightful owner of the cabinet, I protest that my heart began to bleed. I had only been its owner for a month; yet perceive what was the acuteness of my sorrow at its loss! How acute must be the sorrow of the man who probably had been its owner his whole life long, and to whom, not improbably, it had descended as an heirloom through the far-off generations. If I consented to throw the cloak of concealment over the actions of this man Tress, I became a sharer of his crime. It came to me in a flash of instant and indubitable inspiration, that it was my duty, my manifest, my bounden duty to strain every nerve to see that the rightful owner of the Boule Armoire came once more into possession of what was, and had long been, his own. As for the reward which was offered: it was a notable sum. I might fitly apply it to certain purposes of charity which for a considerable period of time I had had in my mind's eye.

No doubt Tress supposed that, in taking away the paper, he had left me without a clue. He was mistaken. He did not know his man. I have an excellent memory of my own. I had the advertisement, every word of it, by heart. Lest a word of it should chance to escape my memory, I sat down and wrote it out upon a sheet of paper.

"So that," I told myself, "no spark of mistaken pity for the sordid wretch whom, once, I imagined was my friend, may steal into my breast to change my righteous purpose, I will go at once to Messrs. Delebat, Dibbs & Gale, and ere an hour is passed I will place them in possession of the information which will enable them to lay the villain low."

I put my hat on there and then. I went out into the street. I called a cab. As I drove towards Lincoln's Inn Fields, I was conscious of a gentle glow of satisfaction as I reflected that, after all, mine would be the nobler part. That it would be mine to unmask, and put a final termination to, a long drawn out career of crime. I flattered myself that I would still be more than even with Mr. Joseph Tress. I had got back my three hundred and seventy pounds—and five shillings for the canvas and the cord. I fancied that he would find that he had bought his bargain dear. Penal servitude for life, he said? Well, we should see if it would be penal servitude for life for him. If it came to the test, I doubted if he would be so willing to be broken on the wheel, even for the sake of being the temporary, and, indeed, momentary possessor of a cabinet by M. Boule. As a matter of fact, my chief fear was that the fellow had some deep laid design, and that, before I could put the police upon his track, he would have spirited the cabinet away, if he himself had not vanished too.

When the cab drew up in front of No. 37, it was this fear which made me spring out of the vehicle with a degree of haste which does not mark my movements, as a rule, but which, on this occasion, was prompted by my anxiety to find myself, as soon as possible, in the presence of Messrs. Delebat, Dibbs & Gale. Hurrying into the house, I glanced at the name-board which was in the hall. I took it for granted that Messrs. Delebat, Dibbs & Gale, was the name and title of an old-established firm of family solicitors, who, probably, had dealings chiefly with the aristocracy, and with such persons as could afford to be the owners of a cabinet by Boule. At a first glance, I did not perceive their name. Nor, at a second glance, did I perceive it either. It was odd. The house was No. 37. I looked up, and saw that there was the number, for all the world to see, upon the door. Again I went through the names, this time slowly and carefully, which were on the board. There was no name on it which in the least resembled Delebat, Dibbs & Gale. I had been wrong in my surmise, and they were new comers, then, after all. I must inquire on which floor their offices were situated. I knocked at the first door I came to.

"Can you tell me," I asked of the clerk whom I found within, "on which floor the offices of Delebat, Dibbs & Gale are situated?"

"What name?"

"Delebat, Dibbs & Gale."

"No one of that name here."

"This is No. 37?"

"Yes, this is 37."

"Then this is the address of Messrs. Delebat, Dibbs & Gale."

"No one of that name here."

He was one of those bumptious young men with whom, I clearly perceived, it was not the slightest use my arguing. If I wanted information, I must simply seek for it elsewhere. I went up to the floor above, and I knocked at a door which I found there. My knock was answered by a shock-headed young man, who, I saw at a glance, was even more bumptious than the one downstairs.

"What name?"

That was how he addressed me—while he was still in the very act of opening the door.

"Can you tell me on which floor are situated the offices of Messrs. Delebat, Dibbs & Gale?"

"What name?"

I repeated it. I was beginning to wish that it had been a little shorter.

"There's no one of that name in this house."

"My dear sir, you must be mistaken. I happen to know that this is their address."

"What are they—solicitors?"

"I believe they are solicitors."

"I've got a law list inside. You can have a look at it if you like. I don't believe there's any one of that name on the list. Anyhow, I'm quite sure there's no firm of that name in the Fields."

I saw that it was no more good arguing with this young man than with the other young idiot downstairs. But I accepted his offer to look through the law list. And he turned out to be right, there was no such name upon it. It was very curious. I had no idea that my memory could have played me such a trick. Owing to my agitation I must have made some extraordinary mistake in the name and title of the firm. But there was still another resource, an equally convenient and an equally satisfactory resource—the police station. I left that shock-headed youth. I went downstairs. I returned to the cab. I told the driver to drive me as quickly as he possibly could to the nearest station-house.

When again the driver stayed his cab, I did not spring from it quite so precipitately as I had done before. To be quite frank, I had become conscious that there might be a certain amount of delicacy about the situation after all. Explanations might be required which I might find a trifle awkward. But as I reflected upon the man's criminal misconduct, the more clearly did I perceive that I ought to allow no personal consideration to prevent justice being done, even though the heavens were to fall. Under no circumstances, if I could help it, should Joseph Tress be suffered to retain possession of that Boule Armoire.

They showed me, as I entered the station-house, to a sort of ticket-hole in the wall. On the other side of it, where the booking-clerk stands, there was an inspector of police—or some person of the kind.

"I have come," I observed, "with reference to the advertisement of the Boule Armoire."

"You have come about what?"

It might have been my imagination, but there seemed to be something in the tone of the inspector's voice which induced me to pause. Had I realised how delicate the matter really was? I set my teeth. At all risks, come what might, I would see the thing well through.

"With reference to the offer of twelve hundred and fifty pounds reward for the recovery of the Boule Armoire. I am in a position to give you information which will lead, not only to the conviction of the thief, but also to the recovery of the stolen property."

The inspector looked at me, and, unless I err, he smiled.

"What's your name?"

"My name at this point of the transaction is immaterial." I felt very strongly that it was. "What you have now to do is to consider the information which I am prepared to place in your possession."

The inspector continued to look at me, and, unless again I err, again he smiled.

"You say you have come with reference to an advertisement?"

"Certainly!" The man's manner began to nettle me. "Don't I tell you that I have come with reference to the advertisement offering twelve hundred and fifty pounds for the recovery of the Boule Armoire?"

"Where did you see this advertisement?"

"Where? In a newspaper."

"What newspaper?"

I hesitated. In my agitation I had omitted to observe the name. I perceived that the inspector's smile was deepening.

"Have you a copy of the paper?"

"I have a copy of the advertisement."

"Will you allow me to look at it?"

I allowed him to look at it. I handed him the sheet of paper on which I had copied out the advertisement from memory. He disappeared with it. If I mistake not he went into an inner room, the door of which I could not see. He kept me waiting his return a most unconscionable time. I began to experience severe discomfort. I was aware of what gross blunders the police are capable. It was within the range of possibility that the man might be making inquiries, which would necessarily be one-sided inquiries, and which might result in his arresting me. I protest that I more than once meditated a retreat. Only I was conscious that the eyes of a policeman, who kept coming in and out, were on me all the time. The inspector's reappearance at the ticket-office, when he at last did reappear, gave me quite a shock, though the words which he immediately proceeded to utter gave me one much greater.

"I think, sir, some one may have been having a jest at your expense. We know nothing of such an advertisement."

He handed me back my sheet of paper. I gasped.

"You know nothing?"

"Nothing." He smiled at my evident amazement. "You might inquire of the firm whose name and address is on your paper."

"No such firm appears to exist."

"No? So I should imagine. Good-day."

Without another word he turned away. As I stood there, with the piece of paper held in my trembling hands, a sudden overwhelming dread came over me. Had I—could I have been—the victim of a monstrous fraud? I knew that there was nothing—no subterfuge, no diabolical contrivance, no ingenious villainy, to which the man Tress would not be willing to resort in order to gain his own nefarious ends. Had he tricked me—robbed me, after all? Plundered me of my Boule Armoire? A mist seemed to come before my eyes. I blundered into the cab.

"Randolph Crescent!" I screamed to the driver. "Drive like the devil, if you can!"

I will do the cabman the justice to admit that he urged his horse to such speed as he could, though not to speed enough for me. I sat within his vehicle, trembling like a child. On reaching Randolph Crescent I thundered at the door. It was opened by the abandoned, badly-trained manservant, whom Joseph Tress, with his wonted, ill-bred familiarity, insisted on calling Bob. I pushed past the fellow without a word. I hurried into the room in which I knew that his master was sure to be.

"You thief!" I cried.

There he was in front of my Boule Armoire. He turned as I came in, and called him by his proper name of thief.

"Pugh, old friend!" He pointed to my cabinet. "I have been having with it such an hour as that first hour which the Passionate Pilgrim spends with his well-won love. Though never had lover so fair a mistress as this sweetheart of mine."

"Give me back the cabinet of which you've swindled me!"

I sprang across the room as if to regain forcible possession of my property. He stood in front of me with a sort of roar.

"What?"

Never did I see a man who was, all at once, in such a rage.

"Dare ever again, within my hearing, to even hint of robbing me of my true love—which is my own, my very own, for ever and for aye—and as I live, I'll not leave in your body a bone whole enough to splinter!"

"That advertisement which you read to me, you yourself put in the paper!"

He was silent for a moment. And he looked at me. And then he laughed. As brutal, as bestial, as ruffian a laugh, as ever yet I heard.

"So you've been to claim the reward?" He laughed again, so long that I thought he would not stop. I even saw him wipe from his eyes the tears which his mirth had caused. "There never was a better joke!" He came and put his hand upon my shoulder, and, showing strength which I never had supposed was his, he shook me so that I began to fear that he would shake me all to pieces. "Why, you Pugh, you're like that Thane of Cawdor, that let I dare not, wait upon I would. You're a rogue in grain, but lack a true rogue's pluck. You'd rob a child, and do it well, but you never would hold up a train. That's where I beat you, Pugh, as the presence of the cabinet in my room is evidence to show. Why, man, directly you had gone behind my back, and played your pretty trick on me, I told myself it did not matter, I'd be sure to best you in the end. So I went to a certain editor I know, a little man, with nothing but a little, struggling suburban paper to yield him bread and cheese; and I told him that if he would insert a certain advertisement in a single copy of a single issue, I'd give him so and so. For him, a monstrous sum. I had my way. The advertisement went in. It appeared in but one single copy. That copy, Pugh, I brought to you. I knew of what stuff you were made, but I never thought you such a cur. I was prepared to carry the fight right through. That advertisement was only to have been the first move in the game. But even at the mere suspicion of an attack, you fell. Poor Pugh! so you robbed the old woman, and I've robbed you; and now that I have your measure, you'll never rob me back again—not you!—so get outside! Your presence desecrates the sanctity of this first sweet hour. It's a discord in the harmony. When the honeymoon is over, now and again you may come back to take a peep at my true love, but—at present, Pugh, I'll conduct you to the door."

That hardened rogue took me by the shoulders. He led me down the stairs. Almost before I had realised the indignity which he was placing on me, I found that I was in the open street. I daresay the cabman, seeing me issue from the house in such a fashion, and perceiving that I stood there in a sort of waking dream, may have wondered if, by chance, his fare was mad. I know that, so far as I was concerned, his voice seemed to come to me from some distant solitude.

"Where shall I drive you, sir?"

"Drive me?" I fell rather than got into his cab. "Drive me home."

THE ADVENTURE OF THE IKON

(MR. TRESS TELLS THE STORY)

CHAPTER I

THE JEW BOY PURSUES

I saw it in a dirty little shop in a dirty little Houndsditch street. The proprietor was a Russian Jew; an ancient man, in ancient rags, and ancient dirt, with anxiety writ large all over him, and eyes which looked at you with that piteous, yearning, glaring something which one sees in the eyes of a famished cur. There seemed to be nothing in the place worth having; merely the sweepings of the lumber-rooms. I penetrated to the back. Hung against the wall, in a recess right at the extremity, was a picture. It was in semi-darkness; the imperfect light made it impossible to guess what the theme might be. I peered closer at it; the subject still remained invisible.

The proprietor, who had hung eagerly on my heels, giving utterance to a curious sound, half whine, half cry, each time I moved, stood and watched me as I peered.

"What do you want for this?" I asked.

For a moment the man was silent; then answered, in a husky, wheezy, servile voice, with an accent which was indescribable:—

"That is an Ikon; a holy picture."

"So? I thought you were a Hebrew."

"That is true; I am a Hebrew. The picture is not mine. It is my wife's."

"Is your wife, then, not of your faith?"

He hesitated.

"Oh, yes, she is of my faith; oh, yes! She is a good woman, my wife."

"I was not aware that among you Hebrews there were such things as Ikons."

The old man was still.

"Did you bring it from Russia?"

"My wife, she brought it from Russia; oh, yes."

"What will you take for it?"

I suddenly became conscious, on turning round, that at the old man's elbow stood a boy; one of those stunted Jew boys, whose ages are not decipherable from their appearance. In size he was but a child; so far as his features went he might have been anything from ten to twenty. His preternaturally sharp features were peering at me through the gloom with what I instinctively felt was marked disfavour. He said something in a foreign language. I at once became persuaded that he was urging the other not to set a price upon the picture. The old man's voice was huskier.

"It is an Ikon. It is my wife's. She is not at home, my wife."

"I'll give you half a sovereign for it." The old man wavered. He would have closed with my offer had not the boy interposed with what sounded to me like a flood of gibberish. The old man listened in silence, plainly troubled by what the youngster said. He re-echoed his own words.

"It is not for me to sell; it is my wife's." For some reason, for which I am unable to account, the lad's interference nettled me. I had not been conscious of any particular desire to possess the thing, but now that the boy, for some cause of which I had not the slightest inkling, was plainly anxious that it should not be mine, I immediately decided that it should be.

"Are you the proprietor of this establishment?"

"I am the proprietor—oh, yes!"

"Then will you be so good as to ask that young gentleman to take himself away. I prefer to deal only with the principal."

The old man spoke to the boy; the boy spoke back. Then both of them began to speak at once, in a foreign tongue, at the top of their voices. I had not the faintest notion what either of them was saying, but if they were not abusing each other, hammer-and-tongs, appearances belied them. Presently the old man passed from words to deeds. He set to buffeting the youngster with a degree of vigour which did him credit. Convinced by force, if not by reason, the youngster retreated to the door. The victor turned again to me.

"Well, will you take that ten shillings?"

"Mein Gott, my friend, do I not tell you it is my wife's? It is not mine to sell!"

"Reserve that sort of thing for some one else. What is it in the shop for, if it is not to sell?—as though there was anything in the place you would not sell. I doubt if the thing's worth twopence, but, as the whim is on me, I'll give you a pound."

"A pound?"

He looked at me with hungry longing. So far as I was able to judge, the whole of his stock would not have fetched much more than a sovereign.

Before he could reply, there came a voice from the door—the voice of the boy. I could not tell what it was he said, but whatever it was it fired his senior with sudden rage. With a scream of passion he made what speed he could to the front. The boy retreated. The old man stood at the entrance, shrieking and gesticulating. Returning, he came nearer to me than was quite agreeable. He almost whispered in my ear:—

"My friend, what I tell you is quite true; it is my wife's. She is very fond of it, my wife; but I tell you what I do. You give me a fair price for it, then I give it all to her; then perhaps she will not be so cross."

"What do you call a fair price? A pound is twenty shillings more than it is worth."

"Oh, my friend, you do not know what you talk about. It is an Ikon, a holy picture. If we were in Russia, a gold mine would not buy it. There is nothing in Russia they value half so much; mein Gott, no!"

"You see, we're not in Russia. I ask you again, what is your idea of a fair price?"

He searched my face with his hungry eyes, trying with might and main to learn to what extent I might be bleedable.

"Ten pounds; that is a very little price."

"Do you think I'm a fool? Keep your picture. I wish you a good day."

He caught at my sleeve as I was going.

"How much you give?"

"I have told you—a pound."

He gasped; then, as I made again as if to go, wheezed out, "Two pounds."

At that moment the boy, reappearing in the doorway, shrieked out some more of his gibberish. I was conscious that as he did so the old man started trembling. That decided me. I produced the required two pounds, and, taking the picture with my own hands from the nail on which it hung, marched out with it into the street. When I got outside I perceived that the boy was eyeing me from the other side of the way. As I walked off I began to be haunted by an uncomfortable feeling that I had behaved like an idiot; to suspect that I had been made the victim of a neat little comedy which had not been performed for the first time for my benefit, nor for the last; to wonder if that ingenuous youth might not have been engaged for the special purpose of inducing a would-be purchaser to imagine that the article which he wished to buy was the one thing which ought not to be sold.

On reaching a thoroughfare which was frequented by omnibuses something occurred, however, which caused me to doubt if, in so suspecting, I might not after all be wrong. Turning to look for a vehicle which journeyed in my direction I saw, only a few paces behind me, that identical boy. That he had followed me was obvious. When I stopped he stopped, and standing still stared at me boldly. Just then an empty hansom came strolling by, and jumping in I drove straight home. The horse was not a bad one, the distance was considerable; yet, as I alighted, the first thing I observed, not fifty yards away, was that selfsame boy. How he had managed to keep the cab in sight was more than I could tell; that he had done so, however, the fact of his presence made evident. I paid and dismissed the cab. As I entered my dining-room I saw through the window the stunted Jew boy stealing past the railings. Pausing at the foot of the steps, he evidently made a mental note of the number which was on the door.

CHAPTER II

THE JEW BOY HAUNTS

During the rest of that day I was engaged. It was the following morning before I was able to give any further attention to my new purchase. I had it in the apartment which I call my study. The room is on the ground floor in the front of the house. I took it out of the cupboard in which I had locked it, and placed it on the table.

"I've been done!"

That was the conclusion at which I arrived almost as soon as I began to examine it. The more I looked at the thing, the stronger my conviction grew. To the best of my knowledge and belief, its intrinsic value would not have justified the expenditure of half a crown. I had been the victim of what, after all, was an old-fashioned trick, and also of my own pig-headedness. As I surveyed it, lying in front of me, I was at a loss to conceive what access of folly could have induced me to buy such rubbish. I had paid two pounds for what, to all intents and purposes, was worth nothing at all.

Whether it was or was not an Ikon, I could not pretend to say. I had seen some curious examples of that variety of fetich—curious, above all things, from an artistic point of view, and in some of Russia's most reverenced places; but I did not remember to have ever seen anything which was quite so bad as that. To begin with, to call it a picture at all seemed absurd— whether "holy" or otherwise. It was not a picture: or, if it were, the artist's original design had become wholly obscured by dirt and grime.

It was about nine inches by twelve. I believe a popular size in Ikons. The so-called picture was in a plain, narrow frame of some dark wood. A border ran round the inside of this frame, of some sort of material which had possibly once been tinsel. Scraps of tinsel seemed to have been stuck on to different parts of the picture itself which favoured the idea that it might, after all, be a veritable Ikon. The Russians have a way of daubing their Ikons, even those which make some pretence to art, with paste and tinsel in a fashion which strikes the outsider as amazing. Some of them are so covered with trumpery—and also, now and then, with jewels—that the pictures themselves are hidden. If the stuff upon my new purchase had been tinsel, then, in spite of appearances, the presumption was that it was an Ikon I had bought.

"This is a case for restoring!" That was what I said to myself, and that was what I felt it to be.

I am acquainted with some of the so-called "secret processes" of the picture-restorers, and, in particular, I am the owner of a recipe for the preparation of a "medium" which is warranted to work wonders with the most hopeless-looking canvases. I always keep some of the stuff on hand—I had some then. I was aware that in the creation of the average Ikon only the coarsest pigments are used—my medium was not likely to do them much harm. I set to work there and then, to arrive if possible at some notion of what the artist's original design had been.

I laid the picture in a good light, flat upon the table. Moistening a fragment of clean sponge, I applied it to the surface of the painting. The moment I did so, to my surprise, smoke began to ascend, exactly from the place where the surface had been moistened. I touched it, thoughtlessly perhaps, with the tip of my finger. To my disgust it burned me—so smartly that, in my hasty withdrawal, the sponge dropped from my hand. The pain was quite acute. My finger-tip had the appearance of having come into contact with some sort of corrosive acid; vitriol could not have taken more immediate effect. Seemingly, I had been doubly tricked. In the ordinary sense, the thing was not a painting at all; unless I was to suppose that it was, in very truth, a "holy" picture, and that I was being punished for my sacrilegious handling.

The moistened place still smoked, and, also, where the sponge had dropped. As I watched, a rather striking little effect took place. As the smoke continued, before my eyes the painting disappeared; until, as it ceased, where it had been nothing but the bare panel remained.

I had been right in my first conclusion: the thing was not a picture at all. The panel had been smeared over with some sort of chemical, which at a cursory inspection looked like oil-colour. My medium, acting as a kind of reagent, had not only detected its presence, it had taken it away. It looked as if I had been the victim of an actual fraud; that I could ever have been so gullible seemed ludicrous.

"I'll see this through. Since the process of restoration has gone so far, it shall go still farther."

Gripping the sponge with a pair of nippers, so as to preclude the possibility of my unprotected flesh coming into unpleasant close contact, I passed it over the entire surface. A thick smoke at once arose. It had a disagreeably pungent odour; its presence in the room became uncomfortably conspicuous. I turned, intending to open the window to let it out. As I did so, who should I see, standing on the other side of the road, but that stunted Jew boy.

"What the devil is he doing there?"

His presence absolutely startled me. If, as I had already concluded, I had been made the victim of a paltry swindle, one would have supposed that, as one of the principals in the business, the young gentleman would have preferred to give my neighbourhood as wide a berth as possible. But it unmistakably was he. He was attired in the same suit of clothes which, small though he was, was three or four sizes too small for him. He wore his battered billycock hat tipped forward at the same disreputable angle, and, with his hands thrust into his breeches' pockets, he stood staring at my premises as if he were a fixture for the day. The impudence of the thing incensed me. It was bad enough to be done, but to be spied upon as well!

I threw the window open.

"Boy!" I cried, "you young rascal, you come here. I want to speak to you!"

He paid not the slightest heed. I might have been addressing the moon for all the notice that he took of me. He continued to stare, reminding me of nothing so much as of a bird of ill-omen.

I went to the hall door. I did not intend, if I could help it, to allow my juvenile friend to have all the fun to himself. But if he had any resemblance to a bird, it was not to the bird which allows itself to be caught with salt. The instant I showed my nose at the door, he took to his heels and ran down the street like the wind; as I watched his pace I understood how it was that he had been able to keep my cab in sight. I saw him vanish round the distant corner; waited some seconds for his reappearance; then, as there seemed no further signs of him, returned indoors.

The smoke had gone, and the painting too. The panel was left as bare of paint as the palm of my hand. That there was nothing on it to burn me now I proved by tangible evidence. Taking it up I endeavoured to peer into the mystery—for that there was more in the situation than met the eye I was beginning to be convinced—jumping, with what some people might call characteristic haste, from conclusion to conclusion. If, yesterday, the boy had not been in earnest in his endeavours to dissuade the old man from parting with his so-called Ikon, then I was not so good a judge of human nature as I supposed myself to be. His whole conduct proclaimed his sincerity—else why had he followed me home, and why had I, at so seemingly apposite a moment, again detected him in the act of espial? What his reasons were was another matter. They might be, so to speak, extraneous, or they might be contained in the thing itself. Which was it? It was a question which I decided that I would, if possible, find an answer to.

I subjected my latest acquisition to a keener scrutiny. There certainly was nothing about it, in its present condition, to recommend it as a possession to any one whatever. It was simply a panel of some dark wood, set in a frame of what looked like bog-oak. There were stains upon it here and there, but, with that exception, my medium had restored it to its natural condition, in a sense I had not intended. I examined the stains through a magnifying-glass. They were excoriations in the grain of the wood, caused probably by the corrosive action of the acid with which it had been smeared. What struck me most was the fact that the panel seemed to be unnecessarily thick. The frame was an inch in thickness, and the panel itself was within a fraction of being flush with the frame, both at the back and the front. It looked as if it were formed of a single piece of wood; indeed, now that the "painting" had gone, it would have been difficult to tell which had been meant for the back and which for the front. Yet, if it did consist of but a single piece of wood, then it was of abnormal lightness. Closer examination suggested that both panel and frame were of oak; either artificial means had been used to stain the frame a darker shade, or it was really older than the panel, but, as viewed through a glass of considerable power, the grain of both seemed to be identical. Oak is not a light wood, especially seasoned oak. If the panel was solid, it ought to have been heavier. I rapped it with my knuckles; but without result. I could not make up my mind whether it did or did not sound hollow. It is not so easy as may be supposed to hold a piece of wood, less than an inch thick, in one's hand, and to judge, by sound alone, of its solidity.

I resolved to take the whole affair to pieces, and had no sooner arrived at the resolution than I discovered something which ought not, previously, to have escaped my observation. The frame itself seemed to have been made out of a single piece of wood. The ordinary picture-frame is, of course, joined at the four corners. If that had been the case with this one, then the work had been uncommonly well executed; with my powerful magnifying-glass I could discover no trace of the joints. It really seemed as if panel and frame had been cut out of the same block.

On the supposition that there was a hollow somewhere in which something was concealed, then there must exist a means of gaining ingress, I went over the whole affair carefully, minutely, with my strong glass, perceiving as a result nothing which pointed to anything of the kind. Only one thing remained for me to do, to enable me to finally satisfy myself that I actually had been done, both by the man and the boy: it but remained for me to break the whole thing up into matchwood. Then I indeed should know that there was nothing, either inside or outside of it, worth having.

I was about to get the tools which would enable me to perform the work of destruction in the most expeditious manner possible, when there came a knock at the hall door; not the authoritative rat-tat-tat of one's equal, but the solitary, deprecating tap of the dependant. Was that boy back again, after his Ikon?

An odd tremor of excitement suddenly possessed me—I am unable to account for it, but it was so. A conviction came to me—unreasonably enough—that there was some strange story associated with the thing, the key to which I would myself unriddle. I had bought and paid for it. If there was any loss to be connected with the transaction, then I was prepared to stand by it. But the thing was mine; if the vendor regretted his bargain, regret would have to be his only solace.

Hurriedly returning the panel to the cupboard, I locked the door and pocketed the key—only just in time. I was moving away from the cupboard, when the door opened to admit my servant.

"There is a woman who wishes to speak to you, sir."

CHAPTER III

THE WOMAN PLEADS

Even while the words were still upon the fellow's lips, there was the woman herself to say so. Not a little, I saw, to the man's surprise—he probably had requested her to wait upon the doorstep. Then came past him into the room somebody who certainly was not the stunted Jew boy.

It was a woman, young—possibly under twenty—and also beautiful. Small and slight, in spite of her disfiguring habiliments I could not doubt that she was graceful. Obviously a Jewess, with the exception of the big, velvety black eyes, which are a hall-mark of the race, her features were as daintily fashioned as any Christian's of them all. Fittingly attired, she might have taken pride of place among her sisters anywhere. As it was, her garments, which, to tell the truth, were not too clean, seemed to have been taken haphazard from the contents of a rag-shop, without the slightest reference to personal fitness. Yet, although they were anything but an adornment, I thought that I never had seen a lovelier face.

When the servant had left us I felt almost awkward. The woman was so childlike, and yet so self-possessed. She stood quite still, and after one keen, quick glance at me, her eyes went wandering eagerly round the room, as if she were taking an inventory of all that it contained. As I watched her, I was struck, in spite of her youth, by the stamp of sorrow which seemed to have been irrevocably branded on her lovely face; and when at last I really met her eyes, they occasioned me a positive thrill. If ever anguish was revealed in human eyes, I saw it in that woman's then.

I broke the silence.

"What is it I can do for you?"

For some moments she did not reply. Again her eyes went wandering eagerly round the room, as if she was looking for something which she could not see. Then she spoke, with an air of being disappointed in her search:—

"It is you who has bought my Ikon?"

In spite of her strong foreign accent, which I make no attempt to reproduce, her voice was not only musical, but it suggested cultivation. Although she spoke softly, it vibrated either with passion or with pain.

"I do not understand you."

I did; but that was by the way. All diplomatists must shuffle.

"You bought my Ikon from my husband."

Her husband! Was it possible that ancient sinner was the husband of this mere child? He looked like her great-great-grandfather.

"It was not his to sell."

"Indeed!"

"Yes, indeed—and again indeed! He told you that it was not his to sell."

"And yet he sold it."

"Yes, he sold it; because, for money, he would sell anything; his wife, his child—himself! But it was mine—mine—mine!" She touched her breasts, quickly, with her two hands. "Levi tells me that you gave two pounds for it—two sovereigns. I bring you back your money."

She held out her right hand; many a girl's is larger. A couple of coins were on the outstretched palm. I declined them with a gesture.

"I do not buy to sell again."

She eyed me as if she did not quite catch my meaning. Her hand trembled. Something seemed to rise in her throat, causing her to gasp for breath. She reiterated her former statement.

"But it is mine—mine—mine!"

"Pardon me, at present it is mine."

Then she did something for which I was unprepared. The emotional impulses of these foreign women take one unawares. Bursting into a passionate flood of weeping, she became, all at once, a small whirlwind of excitement.

"What is it you want? Is it to make money—are you like my husband? See; here are three—four—five pounds." Lifting her skirt, she disclosed, suspended from her waist, a large bag-pocket, such as our mothers used to wear. From this she began to tumble a singular variety of articles out on to my table. "Here is silver—there are three pounds more." She emptied a canvas bag of its contents. "Here are my rings—all of them." The extraordinary creature threw down several rings, which seemed to be radiant with diamonds and gems, and which at any rate were distinctly not of a kind with whose possession one would have credited a person attired as she was. "The rest of my jewellery my husband has, but I will get it for you—all! I will give you everything—everything!—if you will give me back my Ikon."

She presented an amazing spectacle, as she stood there, torn by her sobs, half beside herself with strange excitement, scattering her posses- sions with a carelessness which was so astonishing in a person whose entire costume would probably have been dear at half a sovereign. When I replied to her, my tone was as dry as I could make it. I was becoming more and more convinced that there was a mystery about the thing, which, from ev- ery point of view, it might be well worth my while to solve.

"Before I entertain your proposition, I should like to have some notion why you are making it. It is, to say the least of it, strange that one day I should buy an article from your husband for a couple of pounds, and that the next you should come, and, according to your own statement, offer me everything you possess to buy it back again. I should like to know what has caused this sudden and astounding enhancement of its value."

It was again a second or two before she appeared to altogether grasp my meaning. When she did her countenance changed—she seemed to be a changeable creature. A furtive look came on to her face. She shrank back, glancing, as if nervously, over her shoulder.

"Do I not tell you it is mine?"

"Precisely. But even granting that it was yours, surely that is not a suf- ficient explanation. You do not worship Ikons."

Unless I was mistaken, she made an attempt to regain her courage; enough of it to enable her to make a show of blustering.

"That is my business. What affair is it of yours?"

"If you will consider for a moment, you will perceive that you are making it my affair. May I ask if your husband knows of the visit you are paying me today?"

Her discomfiture obviously increased. Again she glanced over her shoulder, as if fearful that some one was at her back.

"My husband? What has he to do with you?"

"He has this much to do with me, that it was from him that I made the purchase." Pausing, I fixed my gaze on her as impressively as I could. "I shall begin to suspect that there is more about your so-called Ikon than meets the eye; that it contains a secret—a secret which is hidden even from your husband."

There could be no doubt that I had hit the nail—some nail—upon the head. I never saw a creature display such unmistakable signs of terror as she did then. She cowered as if I had struck her some deadly blow. Her great eyes dilated till she seemed all eyes. I feared, for some moments, that she was going to swoon. But she retained sufficient control over herself to prevent her doing that. And after an interval, during which I was in a state of painful nervous tension, she said, in a tone which, although it was but the faintest whisper, affected me more than her hysteric cries had done:—

"Have you seen?"

She kept her gaze fastened upon my face, with what I felt was unconscious strenuousness, as she waited in breathless suspense, as if it were a matter of life and death, for my reply.

"Have I seen what? Your conscience betrays you. There evidently is something to be seen."

Directly I had spoken, she perceived the mistake which she had made.

With what was plainly an effort, she endeavoured to pull herself together. Speaking all at once with feverish volubility, she did her best to lead me to suppose that I had misjudged her.

"It is false! That is not what I meant. There is nothing to see, nothing at all! Only, this Ikon; I have had it all my life. I am in a foreign land; it is the one thing I brought with me from my own country; it is dear to me, very dear! I would not part with it for anything; it is the only thing for which I care! I entreat you to give it back to me. I will give you all I have, only give it back to me. I am alone, my life is sad—very sad! although I am so young. I beg you not to take from me the only thing for which I care!"

She held out her clasped hands to me with a wild abandonment of despair, which, although in striking contrast to the habitudes of our phlegmatic English constitution, I found to be not a little pathetic. For an instant I was disposed to yield to impulse rather than to reason, and to accede to her request. Then, reason prevailing, I turned away. My tone was intentionally frigid:—

"Bring your husband to me, my good woman, and let him show me good grounds why I should return to him that which I have bought and paid for, and neither you nor he will find that I am unreasonable. But, until you do that, you must excuse me if I am unable to believe that in your endeavours to obtain possession of my little purchase you are actuated by the reasons you profess."

"You will not give me back my Ikon?"

"I will not, until your husband, from whom I bought it, shows me sufficient cause."

"I will have it!"

"Indeed! is that the tone you adopt? It is just what I expected." I rang the bell; Bob appeared. "Show this woman into the street, and if she returns at any time alone, refuse to admit her."

"Give me my Ikon! give it me! It's mine—mine—mine!"

Again she broke into a paroxysm of sobs, and also, perhaps, by way of a slight variety, into a paroxysm of what to me was gibberish. For all I knew, she was raining down curses on my head in the unknown tongue in which the man and the boy had spoken to each other the day before. In obedience to a nod from me, Haines touched her on the shoulder.

"Now then, out you go!"

She paused in the middle of what sounded like her diatribe. Her lovely face was transfigured by a conflict of emotions. She looked at Haines, then at me—not lovingly; then she turned to leave the room, apparently oblivious of the rings and money which she had left upon the table. I checked her.

"One moment! You have forgotten your property; be so good as to take it with you."

"I will not! I will not! You have my Ikon, the only thing for which I care—you may have everything else of mine as well!"

"That will not suit me, I assure you—you must be mad! Haines, that property on the table belongs to this woman. Put it in a sheet of paper. If she declines to take it, lay it on the pavement outside the street door. I decline to assume any responsibility for its safety."

Haines gathered the miscellaneous collection together in a sheet of *The Times*. As he did so, I noticed that the woman's eyes were again wandering round the room. She favoured every hole and corner, every nook and cranny, with the shrewdest scrutiny. Nothing could have escaped that insistent vision. Had a trace of the Ikon been visible she would certainly have spotted it. I was uncomfortably conscious that she was carrying away with her a mental plan of the room and its contents, which some day she might use in a fashion I should not relish.

Haines made the sheet of *The Times*, containing her belongings, into a neat parcel. When he had finished—Bob Haines is not what I should call expeditious in his movements—snatching it from his hand she went out of the room and out of the house without a word.

CHAPTER IV

THE SECRET OUT

I did not unlock the cupboard in which I had placed the Ikon until the evening. All through the day I was conscious of a vague sensation of unrest. I was feeling as I fancy the man must feel who has chanced upon something which he would very much like to keep, but which he is doubtful if he ought to. If the man really had sold me what belonged to the woman, then, clearly, I had no moral, or even legal, right to its retention.

"If such is the case, her remedy is easily found. Let her give me some shadow of proof, other than her bare word, and I will disgorge at once."

But in my heart I was aware that that was exactly what she could not, or dared not, do. The secret of the thing, whatever it might be, was hidden from her husband. Rather than make of him her confidant, I knew, from the look of terror which had come upon her face, when I spoke of him, that she would rather sacrifice her property.

That Ikon, like the cucumber in the Ingoldsby "Confession," lay heavy on my breast. It went with me wherever I went. It came between me and the newspaper at the club—between me and the cards at the afternoon rubber. I went with a man to Richmond to dine, with the sole intention of getting the thing out of my mind. But it was no use. As I ate my soup, I asked myself: "I wonder what the secret really is?" With the fish came the query: "Is it prisoned in the panel; and if so, how and where?" I was mentally ringing the changes on this sort of thing all through the meal. I believe that my companion thought I was unwell—and I was unwell. I was momentarily courting indigestion; becoming positively feverish; my nervous system getting completely out of order. I was beginning to fear that I was in for a bilious attack at the very least—at my time of life a man ought not to traffic in mysteries!

But the shock came to me as I was returning to Waterloo by train—came in the form of a query. "Suppose that the secret was political?" Good heavens, suppose that it was! I thought of the stories I had heard of the "underground railway" which exists between England and Russia; of the "Nihilist centres" which are suspected to exist in our midst; of the extraordinary means which they are understood to adopt to convey criminating matter to and from their co-conspirators at home. This woman was a Russian; of a persecuted race; she herself might be a refugee from the Tsar's police. That might explain what one would be justified in calling her unnatural anxiety to get back her Ikon; it might contain that which, if known, would suffice to set the whole of Europe on the alert.

I daresay that Haines, who is an observant man, noticed in my looks some appearance of disorder; but being also a wise man, he did not say so. I asked if any one had called during my absence. He hesitated before he answered:—

"Well, sir, there hasn't been any one called, so to speak, but there's been a nasty little Jew boy hanging about the place all day, and even standing on the steps, as if he was going to call. Once I opened the door to ask him what his little game was, but he took to his heels, and cut like lightning—I never saw any one run so fast. But in a minute he was back again; and only when I was lighting up I saw that he was still hanging about on the other side of the street."

The Jew boy! So a watch had been kept upon my premises. For all I knew, my footsteps had been dogged all day. I was getting up to the neck in mysteries.

Haines went to bed. I went into the study. It was after eleven. I was not only tired, I was out of sorts; but rest was out of the question till I had solved the secret of the Ikon. I knew that, if I went to bed without at least attempting a solution, it would haunt me through the night, banish slumber from my eyes, and not impossibly drag me down to tamper with its intricacies in the small hours of the morning. I was alone; sure not to be disturbed; safe from prying eyes, both from within and without the house. Whatever I found I might conceal.

As I took the Ikon out of the cupboard, I was absolutely conscious of a thrill in the region of the spinal cord. It was in the same condition in which I had left it, which might seem a trite remark to make until one reflected on the interests which might be concerned in causing it to be otherwise. I was bound to admit, as I turned it over and over, and laid it in front of me upon the table, that a more ordinary looking article it would be hard to find. If it actually did contain, say, a clue to Nihilistic wickedness, anything less likely to attract unusual attention from the custom-house authorities or the police could scarcely have been chosen.

Having examined its exterior for about the dozenth time, as minutely as possible, and once more having discovered nothing in any way peculiar, I decided upon my plan of campaign—I would begin by splitting it in two. Turning to take a chisel out of my tool-drawer, my attention was caught by a sound from the street outside: the sound of footsteps on the pavement in front of my house. I listened: all was still. It was probably some passer-by. I got the chisel, and was selecting a place on the panel on which to commence operations, when there came the sound again. Undoubtedly they were the steps of some person who was, apparently, right in front of the window of my room. Was it possible that that young rascal of a Jew boy was playing the spy in the night? I reflected—considered my surroundings. Not only were the blinds lowered, but thick curtains were drawn right across the window in such a way that I knew from experience not a gleam of light was visible from the street without. So far as any one outside could guess, the apartment might have been enveloped in pitchy darkness. The Jew boy might stay there for all the information he could gain.

Yet, as I proceeded, I was aware that the suspicion that some one might still be trying to spy on me had given another fillip to my nerves. I turned the thing over on to what had been its face, and, with the cutting edge of my chisel, began to make an incision in the centre of the back. The wood, as I had foreseen, proved to be almost as hard as metal. Although the tool was sharp, instead of cutting, it scarcely scratched the surface. Leaning, however, suddenly on the handle, with as much of my weight as I could bring to bear, something happened which took one rather aback: the chisel went through the wood as if there had been nothing there. Apparently just there the panel was little more than a skin—as thin as a sheet of paper.

Expecting more resistance, I had used more force than was necessary, and the result was that the unlooked-for descent of the tool had given me quite a jerk. It was a moment before I recovered myself; as I did so, again there came a sound from the street. It was not footsteps this time, but a shuffling sound, as of some one or something slipping. It went as quickly as it came. In the ensuing silence, I heard what seemed to be voices—persons whispering. They might whisper, whoever they were. I was hot on the scent of the secret—in a few seconds it would be mine.

Though the panel might be, as it were, a shell, I could feel, even with the point of my chisel, that the hollow within was filled with something. It might be papers, documents of vital consequence, bank-notes even; it was something yielding. Exactly what it was I would quickly know. I had but to prise the panel open; the contents would be bare. I set about doing it, ripping the wood open as easily, now that my chisel had obtained a purchase, as if it had been so much paper.

While I was engaged in this operation, I was dimly conscious that something unusual was taking place outside my window. But the plain truth is that I was, if you choose, so foolishly absorbed in what I was doing that I had no attention to speak of left for anything else. Another instant or two was all I wanted. Then, when I had seen all that there was to see, it would be time enough to, if necessary, make inquiries elsewhere.

Half the panel came in splinters out of the frame. The other half!—I leaned forward with a degree of excitement of which I scarcely thought that I could have been capable, to see what was beneath. At first I could not make it out at all. There were three or four articles of a character with which I was not familiar. They seemed to have been carefully folded up, so that they might be packed away in the smallest possible compass. What they were or what purpose they were intended to serve, I found it difficult to determine.

I picked one up gingerly between my fingers and my thumb. It was a little thing, apparently of some kind of leather, quaintly fashioned. I regarded it askance, twisting it round and round, glimmerings of comprehension gradually dawning on me. Was it a Lilliputian shoe, of a style and shape with which I was unacquainted? Could it have been meant for a doll—or for a baby? There was another like it; a small frock, made of some fine linen stuff, exquisitely worked with all sorts of dainty devices; a tiny sort of nightcap, which was also covered with beautiful needlework—and that was all. Stay, there was something else! On the other panel there was a picture, roughly done, but evidently by a workman who had some claim to call himself an artist—the picture of a baby's face.

And that was the Ikon!

As I stared, realising with some confusion the unexpected nature of the articles whose hiding-place I had laid bare, feeling almost as if I had been guilty of some sort of sacrilege in breaking into so strange a shrine, there came from the window a snapping sound. I knew, as well as if I had seen it done, that some one outside had inserted a knife or some other sharp implement into the crevice at the top, and with its aid forced back the hasp. I did not move—I waited for developments. They came. I heard the window raised, the rustling of the blind; then the curtain was thrust aside, and a woman's face looked in—the woman of the morning.

Under the circumstances I never encountered any one who behaved more boldly, not to say more impudently. Here was a woman, detected in the act of making a burglarious entry into a house at dead of night, yet, when she perceived its proprietor—as of course she immediately did do—instead of flying for her life, or at least for her liberty, her glance travelled to the contents of the Ikon displayed upon the table, and leaping into the room, as if of right, she snatched up the shoes, and the frock, and the night-cap, and the picture, and, pressing them to her bosom, broke into a tumult of tears, the like of which, before or since, I have never seen or heard.

"It is my baby's; it is my little baby's—it is my own baby's! Mine—mine—mine!"

She stood confronting me, her treasures held tightly to her, as if she were a tiger-cat daring me to rob her of her young. Looking away from her I saw that another face was peeping through the curtains, the face of the stunted Jew boy. To do him justice, he seemed to be more conscious of the heinous nature of his nefarious behaviour than the woman. He was plainly quivering with terror for himself, and with amazement at her audacity. I have no doubt that, if I had made a movement in his direction, he would have vanished in a twinkling, heedless of the plight which he had left her in. When I addressed her, my tone and manner were magisterial.

"If you had told me this morning what the contents of your so-called Ikon really were, I would have returned it to you at once, and so have saved you from the crime which, in consort with your rascally companion, you have now committed. Or a hint from your husband would have been equally efficacious."

"My husband?" Again that look of terror came on her face; again she cowered as if she had been struck a blow. Her voice sank. "He does not know! I had my baby before I knew him, long, long ago—when I was a girl!" (She was scarcely out of her childhood then.) "They took my baby's father for the army, and my baby died, and my parents married me to my husband; they did not let him know that I had had a baby, and I did not dare to tell him, they would have killed me! So I brought with me to England my baby's shoes—oh, the little shoes! and my baby's frock—oh, the little frock! and my baby's cap—oh, the little cap! and my baby's picture—oh, the pretty babe!" Each time this emotional young woman played the part of echo to her own words she covered the various garments with hysterical kisses. "And I said it was my Ikon—and it was my Ikon! God of Abraham, Isaac and of Jacob, Thou knowest it was my Ikon—all for which I cared!"

She fell on her knees beside the table, and, pillowing her head on her treasures, was silent; but whether she prayed, or whether she was doing her best to stem the sobs which were shaking her slender frame, was more than I could say.

* * * *

I compounded a felony, or something very like one. I permitted her to go scot-free, and to take her rubbish with her. I heard some further details of her queer history. She had actually left her old ruffian of a husband fast asleep in bed, and slunk away from his side, and crossed London, and committed a daring burglary, in order to regain possession of a few odds and ends of baby clothing. It seemed that the stunted Jew boy was her brother. He had kept watch and ward on the house to see that the Ikon did not leave it. He had been hanging about the house all day, and she had found him waiting her arrival. He appeared to be a good brother, of a sort; and I am ashamed to say that I let him know I thought so. There is no telling where the young rascal will end. In short, I behaved like an old fool all round.

It is extraordinary in what strange fashions some women who have been mothers do cherish the memory of a little child—beyond a plain bachelor's understanding.

I had to stay in bed the whole of the next day with a bad bilious attack—the worst I had had for months—precisely as I expected. One's follies are sure to find one out somewhere, somehow.

THE ADVENTURE OF THE PUZZLE

(AGAIN MR. TRESS TELLS THE STORY)

CHAPTER I

THE PUZZLE SET

Pugh came into my room holding something wrapped in a piece of brown paper.

"Tress, I have brought you something on which you may exercise your ingenuity." He began, with exasperating deliberation, to untie the string which bound his parcel; he is one of those persons who would not cut a knot to save their lives. The process occupied him the better part of a quarter of an hour. Then he held out the contents of the paper.

"What do you think of that?" he asked.

I thought nothing of it, and I told him so.

"I was prepared for that confession. I have noticed, Tress, that you generally do think nothing of an article which really deserves the attention of a truly thoughtful mind. Possibly, as you think so little of it, you will be able to solve the *puzzle*."

I took what he held out to me. It was an oblong box, perhaps seven inches long by three inches broad.

"Where's the puzzle?" I asked.

"If you will examine the lid of the box, you will see."

I turned it over and over; it was difficult to see which was the lid. Then I perceived that on one side were printed these words:—

"Puzzle: To Open the Box."

The words were so faintly printed that it was not surprising that I had not noticed them at first. Pugh explained.

"I observed that box on a tray outside a secondhand furniture shop. It struck my eye. I took it up. I examined it. I inquired of the proprietor of the shop in what the puzzle lay. He replied that that was more than he could tell me. He himself had made several attempts to open the box, and all of them had failed. I purchased it. I took it home. I have tried, and I have failed. I am aware, Tress, of how you pride yourself upon your ingenuity. I cannot doubt that, if you try, you will not fail."

While Pugh was prosing, I was examining the box. It was at least well made. It weighed certainly under two ounces. I struck it with my knuckles; it *sounded* hollow. There was no hinge; nothing of any kind to show that it ever had been opened, or, for the matter of that, that it ever could be opened. The more I examined the thing, the more it whetted my curiosity. That it could be opened, and in some ingenious manner, I made no doubt— but how?

The box was not a new one. At a rough guess I should say that it had been a box for a good half-century; there were certain signs of age about it which could not escape a practised eye. Had it remained unopened all that time? When opened, what would be found inside? It sounded hollow; prob- ably nothing at all—who could tell?

It was formed of small pieces of inlaid wood. Several woods had been used; some of them were strange to me. They were of different colours; it was pretty obvious that they must all of them have been hard woods. The pieces were of various shapes—hexagonal, octagonal, triangular, square, oblong, and even circular. The process of inlaying had been beautifully done. So nicely had the parts been joined that the lines of meeting were difficult to discover with the naked eye; they had been joined solid, so to speak. It was an excellent example of marquetry. I had been over-hasty in my depreciation; I owned as much to Pugh.

"This box of yours is better worth looking at than I first supposed. Is it to be sold?"

"No, it is not to be sold. Nor"—he "fixed" me with his spectacles—"is it to be given away. I have brought it to you for the simple purpose of as- certaining if you have ingenuity enough to open it."

"I will engage to open it in two seconds—with a hammer."

"I dare say. *I* will open it with a hammer. The thing is to open it with- out."

"Let me see." I began, with the aid of a microscope, to examine the box more closely. "I will give you one piece of information, Pugh. Unless I am mistaken, the secret lies in one of these little pieces of inlaid wood. You push it, or you press it, or something, and the whole affair flies open."

"Such was my own first conviction. I am not so sure of it now. I have pressed every separate piece of wood; I have tried to move each piece in every direction. No result has followed. My theory was a hidden spring."

"But there must be a hidden spring of some sort, unless you are to open it by a mere exercise of force. I suppose the box is empty."

"I thought it was at first, but now I am not so sure of that either. It all depends on the position in which you hold it. Hold it in this position—like this—close to your ear. Have you a small hammer?" I took a small hammer. "Tap it, softly, with the hammer. Don't you notice a sort of reverberation within?"

Pugh was right, there certainly was something within; something which seemed to echo back my tapping, almost as if it were a living thing. I mentioned this to Pugh.

"But you don't think that there is something alive inside the box? There can't be. The box must be air-tight, probably as much air-tight as an exhausted receiver."

"How do we know that? How can we tell that no minute interstices have been left for the express purpose of ventilation?" I continued tapping with the hammer. I noticed one peculiarity, that it was only when I held the box in a particular position, and tapped at a certain spot, that there came the answering taps from within. "I tell you what it is; Pugh, what I hear is the reverberation of some machinery."

"Do you think so?"

"I'm sure of it."

"Give the box to me." Pugh put the box to his ear. He tapped. "It sounds to me like the echoing tick, tick of some great beetle; like the sort of noise which a death watch makes, you know."

Trust Pugh to find a remarkable explanation for a simple fact; if the explanation leans towards the supernatural, so much the more satisfactory to Pugh. I knew better.

"The sound which you hear is merely the throbbing, or the trembling, of the mechanism with which it is intended that the box should be opened. The mechanism is placed just where you are tapping it with the hammer. Every tap causes it to jar."

"It sounds to me like the ticking of a death watch. However, on such subjects, Tress, I know what you are."

"My dear Pugh, give it an extra hard tap, and you will see."

He gave it an extra hard tap. The moment he had done so, he started.

"I've done it now."

"What have you done?"

"Broken something, I fancy." He listened intently with his ear to the box. "No—it seems all right. And yet I could have sworn I had damaged something; I heard it smash."

"Give me the box." He gave it me. In my turn, I listened. I shook the box. Pugh must have been mistaken. Nothing rattled; there was not a sound; the box was as empty as before. I gave a smart tap with the hammer, as Pugh had done. Then there certainly was a curious sound. To my ear, it sounded like the smashing of glass. "I wonder if there is anything fragile inside your precious puzzle, Pugh, and, if so, if we are shivering it by degrees?"

CHAPTER II

THE PUZZLE SOLVED

"What *is* that noise?"

I lay in bed in that curious condition which is between sleep and waking. When, at last, I *knew* that I was awake, I asked myself what it was that had woke me. Suddenly I became conscious that something was making itself audible in the silence of the night. For some seconds I lay and listened. Then I sat up in bed.

"What *is* that noise?"

It was like the tick, tick, tick of some large and unusually clear-toned clock. It might have been a clock, had it not been that the sound was varied, every half-dozen ticks or so, by a sort of stifled screech, such as might have been uttered by some small creature in an extremity of anguish. I got out of bed; it was ridiculous to think of sleep during the continuation of that uncanny shrieking. I struck a light. The sound seemed to come from the neighbourhood of my dressing-table. I went to the dressing-table, the lighted match in my hand, and, as I did so, my eyes fell on Pugh's mysterious box. That same instant there issued, from the bowels of the box, a more uncomfortable screech than any I had previously heard. It took me so completely by surprise that I let the match fall from my hand to the floor. The room was in darkness. I stood, I will not say trembling, listening—considering their volume—to the *eeriest* shrieks I ever heard. All at once they ceased. Then came the tick, tick, tick again. I struck another match, and lit the gas.

Pugh had left his puzzle box behind him. We had done all we could, together, to solve the puzzle. He had left it behind to see what I could do with it alone. So much had it engrossed my attention that I had even brought it into my bedroom, in order that I might, before retiring to rest, make a final attempt at the solution of the mystery. *Now* what possessed the thing?

As I stood, and looked, and listened, one thing began to be clear to me, that some sort of machinery had been set in motion inside the box. How it had been set in motion was another matter. But the box had been subjected to so much handling, to such pressing and such hammering, that it was not strange if, after all, Pugh or I had unconsciously hit upon the spring which set the whole thing going. Possibly the mechanism had got so rusty that it had refused to act at once. It had hung fire, and only after some hours had something or other set the imprisoned motive power free.

But what about the screeching? Could there be some living creature concealed within the box? Was I listening to the cries of some small animal in agony? Momentary reflection suggested that the explanation of the one thing was the explanation of the other. Rust!—there was the mystery. The same rust which had prevented the mechanism from acting at once was causing the screeching now. The uncanny sounds were caused by nothing more nor less than the want of a drop or two of oil. Such an explanation would not have satisfied Pugh; it satisfied me.

Picking up the box, I placed it to my ear.

"I wonder how long this little performance is going to continue? And what is going to happen when it is good enough to cease? I hope"—an uncomfortable thought occurred to me—"I hope Pugh hasn't picked up some pleasant little novelty in the way of an infernal machine. It would be a first-rate joke if he and I had been endeavouring to solve the puzzle of how to set it going."

I don't mind owning that as this reflection crossed my mind I replaced Pugh's puzzle on the dressing-table. The idea did not commend itself to me at all. The box evidently contained some curious mechanism. It might be more curious than comfortable. Possibly some agreeable little device in clockwork. The tick, tick, tick suggested clockwork which had been planned to go a certain time, and then—then, for all I knew, ignite an explosive, and—blow up. It would be a charming solution to the puzzle if it were to explode while I stood there, in my night-shirt, looking on. It is true that the box weighed very little. Probably, as I have said, the whole affair would not have turned the scale at a couple of ounces. But then its very lightness might have been part of the ingenious inventor's little game. There are explosives with which one can work a very satisfactory amount of damage with considerably less than a couple of ounces.

While I was hesitating—I own it!—whether I had not better immerse Pugh's puzzle in a can of water, or throw it out of the window, or call down Bob with a request to at once remove it to his apartment, both the tick, tick, tick, and the screeching ceased, and all within the box was still. If it *was* going to explode, it was now or never. Instinctively I moved in the direction of the door.

I waited with a certain sense of anxiety. I waited in vain. Nothing happened, not even a renewal of the sound.

"I wish Pugh had kept his precious puzzle at home. This sort of thing tries one's nerves."

When I thought that I perceived that nothing seemed likely to happen, I returned to the neighbourhood of the table. I looked at the box askance. I took it up gingerly. Something might go off at any moment for all I knew. It would be too much of a joke if Pugh's precious puzzle exploded in my hand. I shook it doubtfully; nothing rattled. I held it to my ear; there was not a sound. What had taken place? Had the clock-work run down, and was the machine arranged with such diabolical ingenuity that a certain interval was required, after the clockwork had run down, before an explosion could occur? Or had rust caused the mechanism to again hang fire?

"After making all that commotion the thing might at least come open." I banged the box viciously against the corner of the table. I felt that I would almost rather an explosion should take place than that nothing should occur. One does not care to be disturbed from one's sound slumber in the small hours of the morning for a trifle.

"I've half a mind to get a hammer, and try, as they say in the cookery books, another way."

Unfortunately I had promised Pugh to abstain from using force. I might have shivered the box open with my hammer, and then explained that it had fallen, or got trod upon, or sat upon, or something, and so got shattered, only I was afraid that Pugh would not believe me. The man is himself such an untruthful man that he is in a chronic state of suspicion about the truthfulness of others.

"Well, if you're not going to blow up, or open, or something, I'll say good-night."

I gave the box a final rap with my knuckles and a final shake, replaced it on the table, put out the gas, and returned to bed.

I was just sinking again into slumber, when that box began again. It was true that Pugh had purchased the puzzle, but it was evident that the whole enjoyment of his purchase was destined to be mine. It was useless to think of sleep while that performance was going on. I sat up in bed once more.

"It strikes me that the puzzle consists in finding out how it is possible to go to sleep with Pugh's purchase in your bedroom. This is far better than the old-fashioned prescription of cats on the tiles."

It struck me the noise was distinctly louder than before; this applied both to the tick, tick, tick, and the screeching.

"Possibly," I told myself, as I relighted the gas, "the explosion is to come off this time."

I turned to look at the box. There could be no doubt about it; the noise was louder. And, if I could trust my eyes, the box was moving—giving a series of little jumps. This might have been an optical delusion, but it seemed to me that at each tick the box gave a little bound. During the screeches—which sounded more like the cries of an animal in an agony of pain even than before—if it did not tilt itself first on one end, and then on the other, I shall never be willing to trust the evidence of my own eyes again. And surely the box had increased in size; I could have sworn not only that it had increased, but that it was increasing, even as I stood there looking on. It had grown, and still was growing, both broader, and longer, and deeper. Pugh, of course, would have attributed it to supernatural agency; there never was a man with such a nose for a ghost. I could picture him occupying my position, shivering in his night-shirt, as he beheld that miracle taking place before his eyes. The solution which at once suggested itself to me—and which would *never* have suggested itself to Pugh!—was that the box was fashioned, as it were, in layers, and that the ingenious mechanism it contained was forcing the sides at once both upwards and outwards. I took it in my hand. I could feel something striking against the bottom of the box, like the tap, tap, tapping of a tiny hammer.

"This is a pretty puzzle of Pugh's. He would say that that is the tapping of a death watch. For my part, I have not much faith in death watches, *et hoc genus omne*, but it certainly is a curious tapping. I wonder what is going to happen next?"

Apparently nothing, except a continuation of those mysterious sounds. That the box had increased in size I had, and have, no doubt whatever. I should say that it had increased a good inch in every direction, at least half an inch while I had been looking on. But while I stood looking its growth was suddenly and perceptibly stayed; it ceased to move. Only the noise continued.

"I wonder how long it will be before anything worth happening does happen? I suppose something is going to happen; there can't be all this to-do for nothing. If it is anything in the infernal-machine line, and there is going to be an explosion I might as well be here to see it. I think I'll have a pipe."

I put on my dressing-gown. I lit my pipe. I sat and stared at the box. I dare say I sat there for quite twenty minutes when, as before, without any sort of warning, the sound was stilled. Its sudden cessation rather startled me.

"Has the mechanism again hung fire? Or, this time, is the explosion coming off?" It did not come off; nothing came off. "Isn't the box even going to open?"

It did not open. There was simply silence all at once, and that was all. I sat there in expectation for some moments longer. But I sat for nothing. I rose. I took the box in my hand. I shook it.

"This puzzle *is* a puzzle." I held the box first to one ear, then to the other. I gave it several sharp raps with my knuckles. There was not an answering sound, not even the sort of reverberation which Pugh and I had noticed at first. It seemed hollower than ever. It was as though the soul of the box was dead. "I suppose if I put you down, and extinguish the gas and return to bed, in about half an hour or so, just as I am dropping off to sleep, the performance will be recommenced. Perhaps the third time will be lucky."

But I was mistaken—there was no third time. When I returned to bed that time I returned to sleep, and I was allowed to sleep; there was no continuation of the performance, at least so far as I know. For no sooner was I once more between the sheets than I was seized with an irresistible drowsiness, a drowsiness which so mastered me that I—I imagine it must have been instantly—sank into slumber which lasted till long after day had dawned. Whether or not any more mysterious sounds issued from the bowels of Pugh's puzzle is more than I can tell. If they did, they did not succeed in rousing me.

And yet, when at last I did wake, I had a sort of consciousness that my waking had been caused by something strange. What it was I could not surmise. My own impression was that I had been awoke by the touch of a person's hand. But that impression must have been a mistaken one, because, as I could easily see by looking round the room, there was no one in the room to touch me.

It was broad daylight. I looked at my watch; it was nearly eleven o'clock. I am a pretty late sleeper as a rule, but I do not usually sleep as late as that. That scoundrel Bob would let me sleep all day without thinking it necessary to call me. I was just about to spring out of bed, with the intention of ringing the bell so that I might give Bob a piece of my mind for allowing me to sleep so late, when my glance fell on the dressing-table on which, the night before, I had placed Pugh's puzzle. It *had* gone!

CHAPTER III

A FORTUNE AT A FIND

Its absence so took me by surprise that I ran to the table. It had gone. But it had not gone far; it had gone to pieces! There were the pieces lying where the box had been. The puzzle had solved itself. The box was open—open with a vengeance, one might say. Like that unfortunate Humpty Dumpty, who, so the chroniclers tell us, sat on a wall, surely "all the king's horses and all the king's men" never could put Pugh's puzzle together again! The marquetry had resolved itself into its component parts. How those parts had ever been joined was a mystery. They had been laid upon no foundation, as is the case with ordinary inlaid work. The several pieces of wood were not only of different shapes and sizes, but they were as thin as the thinnest veneer; yet the box had been formed by simply joining them together. The man who made that box had been possessed of ingenuity worthy of a better cause.

I perceived how the puzzle had been worked. The box had contained an arrangement of springs which, on being released, had expanded themselves in different directions until their mere expansion had rent the box to pieces. There were the springs, lying amidst the ruin they had caused.

There was something else amidst that ruin besides those springs; there was a small piece of writing-paper. I took it up. On the reverse side of it was written, in a minute, crabbed hand, "A Present For You." What was a present for me? I looked, and, not for the first time since I had caught sight of Pugh's precious puzzle, could scarcely believe my eyes.

There, poised between two upright wires, the bent ends of which held it aloft in the air, was either a piece of glass, or—a crystal. The scrap of writing-paper had exactly covered it. I understood what it was, which, when Pugh and I had tapped with the hammer, had caused the answering taps to proceed from within. Our taps had caused the wires to oscillate, and in these oscillations the crystal, which they held suspended, had touched the side of the box.

I looked again at the piece of paper. "A Present For You." Was *this* the present—this crystal? I regarded it intently. "It *can't* be a diamond."

The idea was ridiculous, absurd. No man in his senses would place a diamond inside a twopenny-halfpenny puzzle box. The thing was as big as a walnut! And yet—I am a pretty good judge of precious stones—if it was not an uncut diamond it was the best imitation I had seen. I took it up. I examined it closely. The more closely I examined it, the more my wonder grew.

"It *is* a diamond!"

And yet the idea was too preposterous for credence. Who would present a diamond as big as a walnut with a trumpery puzzle? Besides, all the diamonds which the world contains of that size are almost as well known as the Koh-i-noor.

"If it is a diamond, it is worth—it is worth——Heaven only knows what it isn't worth, if it's a diamond."

I regarded it through a strong pocket lens. As I did so I could not restrain an exclamation.

"The world to a China orange, it *is* a diamond!"

The words had scarcely escaped my lips than there came a tapping at the door.

"Come in!" I cried, supposing it was Bob. It was not Bob, it was Pugh. Instinctively I put the lens and the crystal behind my back. At sight of me in my night-shirt Pugh began to shake his head.

"What hours, Tress, what hours! Why, my dear Tress, I've breakfasted, read the papers and my letters, come all the way from my house here, and you're not up!"

"Don't I look as though I were up?"

"Ah, Tress! Tress!" He approached the dressing-table. His eye fell upon the ruins. "What's this?"

"That's the solution to the puzzle."

"Have you solved it, fairly, Tress?"

"It has solved itself. Our handling, and tapping, and hammering must have freed the springs which the box contained, and during the night, while I slept, they have caused it to come open."

"While you slept? Dear me! How strange! And—what are these?"

He had discovered the two upright wires on which the crystal had been poised.

"I suppose they're part of the puzzle."

"And was there anything in the box? What's this?" He picked up the scrap of paper; I had left it on the table. He read what was written on it. "'A Present For You'; what's it mean? Tress, was this in the box?"

"It was."

"What's it mean about a present? Was there anything in the box besides?"

"Pugh, if you will leave the room I shall be able to dress; I am not in the habit of receiving quite such early calls, or I should have been prepared to receive you. If you will wait in the next room, I will be with you as soon as I'm dressed. There is a little subject in connection with the box which I wish to discuss with you."

"A subject in connection with the box? What is the subject?"

"I will tell you, Pugh, when I have performed my toilet."

"Why can't you tell me now?"

"Do you propose, then, that I should stand here shivering in my shirt while you are prosing at your ease? Thank you; I am obliged, but I decline. May I ask you once more, Pugh, to wait for me in the adjoining apartment?"

He moved towards the door. When he had taken a couple of steps, he halted.

"I—I hope, Tress, that you're—you're going to play no tricks on me."

"Tricks on you! Is it likely that I am going to play tricks upon my oldest friend?"

When he had gone—he vanished, it seemed to me, with a somewhat doubtful visage—I took the crystal to the window. I drew the blind. I let the sunshine fall on it. I examined it again, closely and minutely, with the aid of my pocket lens. It *was* a diamond; there could not be a doubt of it. If, with my knowledge of stones, I was deceived, then I was deceived as never man had been deceived before. My heart beat faster as I recognised the fact that I was holding in my hand what was, in all probability, a fortune for a man of moderate desires. Of course, Pugh knew nothing of what I had discovered, and there was no reason why he should know. Not the least! The only difficulty was that if I kept my own counsel, and sold the stone and utilised the proceeds of the sale, I should have to invent a story which would account for my sudden accession to fortune. Pugh knows almost as much of my affairs as I do myself. That is the worst of these old friends!

When I joined Pugh I found him dancing up and down the floor like a bear upon hot plates. He scarcely allowed me to put my nose inside the door before attacking me.

"Tress, give me what was in the box."

"My dear Pugh, how do you know that there was something in the box to give you?"

"I know there was!"

"Indeed! If you know that there was something in the box, perhaps you will tell me what that something was."

He eyed me doubtfully. Then, advancing, he laid upon my arm a hand which positively trembled.

"Tress, you—you wouldn't play tricks on an old friend."

"You are right, Pugh, I wouldn't. Though I believe there have been occasions on which you have had doubts upon the subject. By the way, Pugh, I believe that I am the oldest friend you have."

"I—I don't know about that. There's—there's Brasher."

"Brasher! Who's Brasher? You wouldn't compare my friendship to the friendship of such a man as Brasher? Think of the tastes we have in common, you and I. We're both collectors."

"Ye—es, we're—we're both collectors."

"I make my interests yours, and you make my interests mine. Isn't that so, Pugh?"

"Tress, what—what was in the box?"

"I will be frank with you, Pugh. If there had been something in the box, would you have been willing to go halves with me in my discovery?"

"Go halves! In your discovery! Tress! Give me what is mine!"

"With pleasure, Pugh, if you will tell me what is yours."

"If—if you don't give me what was in that box I'll—I'll send for the police."

"Do! Then I shall be able to hand them what was in the box, in order that it may be restored to its proper owner."

"Its proper owner! I'm its proper owner!"

"Excuse me, but I don't understand how that can be; at least, until the police have made inquiries. *I* should say that the proper owner was the person from whom you purchased the box, or, more probably, the person from whom he purchased it, and by whom, doubtless, it was sold in ignorance, or by mistake. Thus, Pugh, if you will only send for the police, we shall earn the gratitude of a person of whom we never heard in our lives—I for discovering the contents of the box, and you for returning them."

As I said this, Pugh's face was a study. He gasped for breath. He actually took out his handkerchief to wipe his brow.

"Tress, I—I don't think you need use a tone like that to me. It isn't friendly. What—what was in the box?"

"Let us understand each other, Pugh. If you don't hand over what was in the box to the police, I go halves."

Pugh began to dance about the floor.

"What a fool I was to trust you with the box! I knew I couldn't trust you." I said nothing. I turned and rang the bell. "What's that for?"

"That, my dear Pugh, is for breakfast, and, if you desire it, for the police. You know, although you have breakfasted, I haven't. Perhaps, while I am breaking my fast, you would like to summon the representatives of law and order." Bob came in. I ordered breakfast. Then I turned to Pugh. "Is there anything you would like?"

"No, I—I've breakfasted."

"It wasn't of breakfast I was thinking. It was of—something else. Bob is at your service, if, for instance, you wish to send him on an errand."

"No, I want nothing. Bob can go." Bob went. Directly he was gone, Pugh turned to me. "You shall have half. What was in the box?"

"I shall have half?"

"You shall!"

"I don't think it is necessary that the terms of our little understanding should be expressly embodied in black and white. I fancy that, under the circumstances, I can trust you, Pugh. I believe that I am capable of seeing that, in this matter, you don't do me. That was in the box."

I held out the crystal between my finger and thumb.

"What is it?"

"That is what I desire to learn."

"Let me look at it."

"You are welcome to look at it where it is. Look at it as long as you like, and as closely."

Pugh leant over my hand. His eyes began to gleam. He is himself not a bad judge of precious stones, is Pugh.

"It's—it's—Tress!—is it a diamond?"

"That question I have already asked myself."

"Let me look at it! It will be safe with me! It's mine!"

I immediately put the thing behind my back.

"Pardon me, it belongs neither to you nor to me. It belongs, in all probability, to the person who sold that puzzle to the man from whom you bought it—perhaps some weeping widow, Pugh, or hopeless orphan—think of it. Let us have no further misunderstanding upon that point, my dear old friend. Still, because you are my dear old friend, I am willing to trust you with this discovery of mine, on condition that you don't attempt to remove it from my sight, and that you return it to me the moment I require you."

"You're—you're very hard on me." I made a movement towards my waistcoat pocket. "I'll return it you!"

I handed him the crystal, and with it I handed him my pocket lens.

"With the aid of that glass I imagine that you will be able to subject it to a more acute examination, Pugh."

He began to examine it through the lens. Directly he did so, he gave an exclamation. In a few moments he looked up at me. His eyes were glistening behind his spectacles. I could see he trembled.

"Tress, it's—it's a diamond, a Brazil diamond. It's worth a fortune!"

"I'm glad you think so."

"Glad I think so! Don't you think that it's a diamond?"

"It appears to be a diamond. Under ordinary conditions I should say, without hesitation, that it was a diamond. But when I consider the circumstances of its discovery, I am driven to doubts. How much did you give for that puzzle, Pugh?"

"Ninepence; the fellow wanted a shilling, but I gave him ninepence. He seemed content."

"Ninepence! Does it seem reasonable that we should find a diamond, which, if it is a diamond, is the finest stone I ever saw and handled, in a ninepenny puzzle? It is not as though it had got into the thing by accident; it had evidently been placed there to be found, and, apparently, by any one who chanced to solve the puzzle; witness the writing on the scrap of paper."

Pugh re-examined the crystal.

"It is a diamond! I'll stake my life that it's a diamond!"

"Still, though it be a diamond, I smell a rat!"

"What do you mean?"

"I strongly suspect that the person who placed that diamond inside that puzzle intended to have a joke at the expense of the person who discovered it. What was to be the nature of the joke is more than I can say at present, but I should like to have a bet with you that the man who compounded that puzzle was an ingenious practical joker. I may be wrong, Pugh; we shall see. But, until I have proved the contrary, I don't believe that the maddest man that ever lived would throw away a diamond worth, apparently, shall we say £1000?"

"£1000! This diamond is worth a good deal more than £1000."

"Well, that only makes my case the stronger; I don't believe that the maddest man that ever lived would throw away a diamond worth more than £1000 with such utter wantonness as seems to have characterised the action of the original owner of the stone which I found in your ninepenny puzzle, Pugh."

"There have been some eccentric characters in the world, some very eccentric characters. However, as you say, we shall see. I fancy that I know somebody who would be quite willing to have such a diamond as this, and who, moreover, would be willing to pay a fair price for its possession; I will take it to him and see what he says."

"Pugh, hand me back that diamond."

"My dear Tress, I was only going—"

Bob came in with the breakfast tray.

"Pugh, you will either hand me that at once, or Bob shall summon the representatives of law and order."

He handed me the diamond. I sat down to breakfast with a hearty appetite. Pugh stood and scowled at me.

"Joseph Tress, it is my solemn conviction, and I have no hesitation in saying so in plain English, that you're a thief."

"My dear Pugh, it seems to me that we show every promise of becoming a couple of thieves."

"Don't bracket me with you!"

"Not at all, you are worse than I. It is you who decline to return the contents of the box to its proper owner. Put it to yourself, you have *some* common sense, my dear old friend!—do you suppose that a diamond worth more than £1000 is to be *honestly* bought for ninepence?"

He resumed his old trick of dancing about the room.

"I was a fool ever to have let you have the box! I ought to have known better than to have trusted you; goodness knows you have given me sufficient cause to mistrust you! Over and over again! Your character is only too notorious! You have plundered friend and foe alike—friend and foe alike! As for the rubbish which you call your collection, nine-tenths of it, I know as a positive fact, you have stolen out and out."

"Who stole my Sir Walter Raleigh pipe? Wasn't it a man named Pugh?"

"Look here, Joseph Tress!"

"I'm looking."

"Oh, it's no good talking to you, not the least! You're—you're dead to all the promptings of conscience! May I inquire, Mr. Tress, what it is you propose to do?"

"I *propose* to do nothing, except summon the representatives of law and order. Failing that, my dear Pugh, I had some faint, vague, very vague idea of taking the contents of your ninepenny puzzle to a certain firm in Hatton Garden, who are dealers in precious stones, and to learn from them if they are disposed to give anything for it, and if so, what."

"I shall come with you."

"With pleasure, on condition that you pay the cab."

"I pay the cab! I will pay half."

"Not at all. You will either pay the whole fare, or else I will have one cab and you shall have another. It is a three-shilling cab fare from here to Hatton Garden. If you propose to share my cab, you will be so good as to hand over that three shillings before we start."

He gasped, but he handed over the three shillings. There are few things I enjoy so much as getting money out of Pugh!

On the road to Hatton Garden we wrangled nearly all the way. I own that I feel a certain satisfaction in irritating Pugh, he is such an irritable man. He wanted to know what I thought we should get for the diamond.

"You can't expect to get much for the contents of a ninepenny puzzle, not even the price of a cab fare, Pugh."

He eyed me, but for some minutes he was silent. Then he began again:—

"Tress, I don't think we ought to let it go for less than—than five thousand pounds."

"Seriously, Pugh, I doubt whether, when the whole affair is ended, we shall get five thousand pence for it, or for the matter of that, five thousand farthings."

"But why not? Why not? It's a magnificent stone—magnificent—I'll stake my life on it."

I tapped my breast with the tips of my fingers.

"There's a warning voice within my breast that ought to be in yours, Pugh! Something tells me, perhaps it is the unusually strong vein of common sense which I possess, that the contents of your ninepenny puzzle will be found to be a magnificent do—an ingenious practical joke, my friend."

"I don't believe it."

But I think he did; at any rate, I had unsettled the foundations of his faith.

We entered the Hatton Garden office side by side; in his anxiety not to let me get before him, Pugh actually clung to my arm. The office was divided into two parts by a counter which ran from wall to wall. I advanced to a man who stood on the other side of this counter.

"I want to sell you a diamond."

"*We* want to sell you a diamond," interpolated Pugh.

I turned to Pugh. I "fixed" him with my glance.

"I want to sell you a diamond. Here it is. What will you give me for it?"

Taking the crystal from my waistcoat pocket, I handed it to the man on the other side of the counter. Directly he got it between his fingers, and saw what it was that he had got, I noticed a sudden gleam come into his eyes.

"This is—this is rather a fine stone."

Pugh nudged my arm.

"I told you so." I paid no attention to Pugh.

"What will you give me for it?"

"Do you mean, what will I give you for it cash down upon the nail?"

"Just so—what will you give me for it cash down upon the nail?"

The man turned the crystal over and over in his fingers.

"Well, that's rather a large order. We don't often get a chance of buying such a stone as this across the counter. What do you say to—well—to £10,000?"

£10,000! It was beyond my wildest imaginings. Pugh gasped. He lurched against the counter.

"£10,000!" he echoed.

The man on the other side glanced at him, I thought, a little curiously.

"If you can give me references, or satisfy me in any way as to your *bona fides*, I am prepared to give you for this diamond an open cheque for £10,000, or, if you prefer it, the cash instead."

I stared; I was not accustomed to see business transacted on quite such lines as those.

"We'll take it," murmured Pugh; I believe he was too much overcome by his feelings to do more than murmur. I interposed.

"My dear sir, you'll excuse my saying that you arrive very rapidly at your conclusions. In the first place, how can you make sure that is a diamond?"

The man behind the counter smiled.

"I should be very ill-fitted for the position which I hold if I could not tell a diamond directly I get a sight of it, especially such a stone as this."

"But have you no tests you can apply?"

"We have tests which we apply in cases in which doubt exists, but in this case there is no doubt whatever. I am as sure that this is a diamond as I am sure that it is air I breathe. However, here is a test."

There was a wheel close by the speaker. It was worked by a treadle. It was more like a superior sort of travelling tinker's grindstone than anything else. The man behind the counter put his foot upon the treadle. The wheel began to revolve. He brought the crystal into contact with the swiftly revolving wheel. There was a s—s—sh! And, in an instant, his hand was empty; the crystal had vanished into air.

"Good heavens!" he gasped. I never saw such a look of amazement on a human countenance before. "It's splintered!"

CHAPTER IV

AN ILLUSTRATION OF THE HUMOROUS

It *was* a diamond, although it *had* splintered. In that fact lay the point of the joke. The man behind the counter had not been wrong; examination of such dust as could be collected proved that fact beyond a doubt. It was declared by experts that the diamond, at some period of its history, had been subjected to intense and continuing heat. The result had been to make it as brittle as glass.

There could be no doubt that its original owner had been an expert, too. He knew where he got it from, and he probably knew what it had endured. He was aware that, from a mercantile point of view, it was worthless; it could never have been cut. So, having a turn for humour of a peculiar kind, he had devoted days, and weeks, and possibly months, to the construction of that puzzle. He had placed the diamond inside, and he had enjoyed, in anticipation and in imagination, the Alnaschar visions of the lucky finder.

Pugh blamed me for the catastrophe. He said, and still says, that if I had not, in a measure, and quite gratuitously, insisted on a test, the man behind the counter would have been satisfied with the evidence of his organs of vision, and we should have been richer by £10,000. But I satisfy my conscience with the reflection that what I did at any rate was honest, though, at the same time, I am perfectly well aware that such a reflection gives Pugh no sort of satisfaction.

THE ADVENTURE OF LADY WISHAW'S HAND

(MR. PUGH TELLS THE STORY)

CHAPTER I

THE LEGACY

It was a woman's hand. In life, in its proper place at the end of a woman's arm, I could easily believe that it had been beautiful. But as it lay before me on the table, amidst the heap of papers in which it had been wrapped, I am bound to say that it was not its beauty that struck me first of all. One peculiar feature about it was its extraordinary state of preservation. Some embalming process must have been employed with which I was wholly unacquainted. It looked as if it were alive. Not only so!—when, after some not inconsiderable amount of hesitation, I ventured to pick it up, it felt warm to the touch. Almost unwittingly, I pressed it—as I might have pressed a friendly hand in greeting. It seemed to return my pressure. Of course, it was all imagination. But it was imagination of rather a ghastly kind. So vivid was the delusion, that I let it fall back on the table with a start that was sufficiently real.

The hand had been severed, with what had evidently been some sharp instrument, just above the wrist. A joint or some fraction of the bone—I am no anatomist—had apparently been withdrawn, so that the skin overlapped at the end. A white skin it was. I never saw a whiter. Yet it was not a bloodless white. Indeed, it was not difficult to believe that the warm blood was circulating underneath. It was a little hand. It struck me as being exquisitely shaped. A dainty hand. The fingers were long and slender, and tapered to a point. The finger-nails were perfect. They were pink, as are the finger-nails of some young girls. It was those almond-shaped, pink, well-kept finger-nails, which, as much as anything else, gave to the hand such a curious semblance of life. The fingers and thumb were close together, so that, as it lay palm downwards the thumb was in the air, and only the finger-tips pressing against the table, the whole hand formed a sort of arch. It was a right hand. On the fore-finger was a ring. So quaint a ring that, in itself, it was a curio. It was of plain gold, clumsily fashioned, and at the back it had been beaten out by some unskilled craftsman into what had probably been intended to represent a heart-shaped shield. On it were some roughly graven words, which, at any rate without a microscope, I was unable to decipher. I attributed the ring at a rough and ready estimate to perhaps the latter portion of the fourteenth century. It seemed odd to see that ill-shaped and ancient gewgaw on the pretty finger of that dainty little hand.

It was an extraordinary legacy, even for a collector to receive. It appeared that it was a legacy—this woman's hand. From a man, too, who had been but a shadowy acquaintance. It had reached me by a singularly matter-of-fact route—the parcels post. I wondered if the post office officials would have said anything if they had known what it was that they were carrying. With it had come a letter, in which David Wishaw informed me that his brother, Colin, was dead, of which fact I had known nothing, and cared, if possible, still less; and that it had been one of Colin's very last requests that the hand which, according to David, had been known in the family as "Lady Wishaw's hand," should be sent me as a legacy. Very kind of Colin, and also of David, on my honour! David went on to say that Colin had been aware that I was a great collector of curiosities, and he had felt very strongly that "Lady Wishaw's hand" was a curiosity that I should value. Had he indeed! Kinder still, and kinder! The hand, said David, had been an heirloom in the family. Then what on earth did the man mean by passing his family heirlooms on to me, an almost utter stranger? It had been in the family, in uninterrupted sequence, since 1382. When I read that, I wondered whether the man took me for an idiot. The hand—that hand which was lying before me on the table—had been in his family, or anybody's family, since 1382! I doubted very much if it had not been upon a living woman's arm, certainly, within the last six months.

What was I to do with such a legacy? I might be a collector of curiosities, a virtuoso, or a bric-a-brac hunter, which you please. But I was not a curator of an anatomical museum. The curiosities which I collected did not include detached portions of the human frame. The Messrs. Colin and David Wishaw seemed both of them to have laboured under the same misapprehension. I knew a man who collected the ropes with which criminals had been hung. He was a virtuoso of a kind which I was not. Mr. Colin Wishaw should have bequeathed and Mr. David Wishaw should have despatched—by means of parcels post—this curiosity to him.

The ring on the finger did seem more in my way. Getting a magnifying glass, I endeavoured to make out the legend which was on the shield. The ring was old—there could be no doubt about that. It might date from 1382. The legend, in the first place, had been ill done, and in course of time it had become so worn that even with the aid of a good glass, it was difficult to decipher.

"I take myne owne," that's what it is, I finally decided. "It's either 'seke' or 'take'. I fancy it's 'take'—'I take myne owne'. I wonder if that is the motto of the Wishaws? I have a good mind to write to Mr. David Wishaw, and to send him back the hand, and to tell him that, with his permission, as a mark of my appreciation of his brother's thought for me, I'll keep the ring. I might add that, in my judgment, it would be as well if the hand were decently interred. Let's see if I can take the ring off the lady's finger, so that I can have a look at it at closer quarters."

With this idea and with the intention of putting the idea into execution, I once more picked up the hand—though I own I touched it with reluctance. Holding it with my left hand, grasping the ring with the fingers of my right, I prepared to work it loose. Instantly the hand shut up! It was clenched into a fist! I do not think I ever was so startled in my life. The action was so natural, so lifelike, that, though I was in my own drawing-room, and it was broad day, and there was no one present but the hand and myself, it seemed almost as if my heart had leapt into my mouth. It was no optical delusion— the open hand had become a tightened fist. No doubt, it was owing to some muscular contraction—but it was muscular contraction of a sort I did not like. So startled was I that for some moments I could do nothing else but stare. When I could I dropped the hand as if it had been a red-hot coal. I sprang to my feet.

"I'll send it back to Mr. David Wishaw, directly after lunch, ring and all!"

I was momentarily expecting lunch to be announced. It would not do to leave the hand lying on the table open. So I hurriedly caught up the papers in which it had come, and, wrapping them about it anyhow, I put it in a cabinet which stood upon a small side table.

CHAPTER II

THE LEGEND

As I was finishing lunch, there came a knock at the hall door. Nalder went to see who it was. Nalder is a most excellent servant; one whom scarcely anything would induce to forget his place. Therefore, I was the more surprised, when, after a few minutes' absence, he reappeared with an expression of countenance which suggested both bewilderment and pain. He was rubbing his thigh, too, in a manner which, considering that he was standing in the presence of his master, was highly unbecoming.

"What's the matter, Nalder?"

"Well, sir, it's Mr. Brasher, sir."

"Mr. Brasher? What do you mean? What's the matter with Mr. Brasher?"

"Well, sir—nothing's the matter with Mr. Brasher, that I am aware of but—a most extraordinary thing has happened. At least, I beg your pardon, sir, it seems to me a most extraordinary thing. When I showed Mr. Brasher up into the drawing-room, I noticed that the ormolu-cabinet which stands on the Chippendale tripod table was open." This was the cabinet in which I placed Mr. Colin Wishaw's legacy. I must unintentionally have omitted to close it when I left the room. "I went to shut it, and directly I had done so, just as I was turning round, some one or something caught me in the fleshy part of the leg, and gave me such a nip, that, I do believe, there's a piece nipped out."

"Some one or something? What do you mean by some one or something?"

"I don't know, sir, I really don't. There was no one or nothing, near me, that I could see, and that's why I say it's a most extraordinary thing. But I never did feel anything so painful—never."

I left Nalder still rubbing his thigh in a manner which his previous conduct had certainly given me no reason to expect from him. When I went upstairs I found Martin Brasher standing in the centre of the room with a look on his face which might have been twin brother to the look I had seen on Nalder's.

"Pugh," was his salutation to me as I went in, "what on earth have you got in this room of yours?"

"I have a good many things in this room of mine, as, if you had eyes, you would be able to see. What is the matter with you?"

"Upon my word, I hardly know what is the matter with me. Do you know, I was just sitting on that armchair, waiting for you, when something—it felt like somebody's finger-nails—scratched my cheek from top to bottom. Isn't there a scratch to be seen?"

There was, unmistakably. On his left cheek there was what was, obviously, the mark of a recent scratch.

"You've been in dreamland, Brasher, and scratched yourself in your dream."

"Nothing of the kind. I tell you what, Pugh, it's uncommonly queer! But never mind about that now; I have come to tell you that I've got a case at last."

"A case of what?"

"A case for the society—a genuine ghost. Have you ever heard of a man named Wishaw?" I had very much indeed, and very recently. But he didn't give me a chance. He was so very full of his subject, that he went dashing on, without noticing that he had not afforded me an opportunity to answer.

"They're a Scotch family, the Wishaws—one of those Scotch families which antedate the deluge. They have had some peculiar characters among them in their time, more peculiar than pleasant—as some of these Scotch families have had a way of having. One of the most peculiar was a woman, who lived somewhere about the close of the fourteenth century—a propitious period, especially in Scotland, for peculiar characters. She is known among them to this day, as 'Lady Wishaw'. You know how they have that sort of thing in stories. She was the most beautiful woman that ever was— that's of course. She was, also, the wickedest woman that ever was—that's equally of course. She does appear to have done something to deserve a niche, as the latter, in the temple of fame. She was a thief. Such a thief that she became notorious as a thief, even in that age and land of thieves. She stole from foes and friends alike. At last, in the house of a friend, she was caught redhanded, in some more astounding theft than usual. We should have called her a kleptomaniac, I suspect, in these latter days. The term was not invented then, nor the thing. To her host she appeared to have been guilty of an act of hideous treachery. Taking upon himself, as was not uncommon in those sweet and simple days, the offices of judge, jury and executioner, there and then he hacked off her hand at the wrist. The first intimation which the Wishaws received of the latest *petit faux pas* in which the lady had indulged came to them in rather grisly fashion. The lady's guilty, but, I understand, lovely member was sent to them by the host and by a special messenger. The lady herself they never saw again—at least in life. She felt, when she had lost her hand, that she had lost all that there was worth living for. She destroyed herself within the hour. Thus, as you perceive, there was ample ground why a pleasant little feud should exist, henceforth, between the whilom friends, the Wishaws and the Macfies— the host's name was, it seems, Macfie.

"The story goes that the dismembered lady managed to convey some sort of spiritual intimation to her relatives, to the effect that they were never to cease from killing while a Macfie still remained to cumber the ground. Thenceforward, the first end and aim of the Wishaws was to kill the Macfies. And in order that they might not forget their high calling, a special injunction was laid on them that they were to keep the hacked-off hand ever with them as a sort of heirloom, and as a perpetual reminder, until the last of the Macfies was slain. Not only so. They were given clearly to understand, that should a Wishaw arise who, before the Macfies were wholly exterminated, proved unworthy, and ceased from killing, the dead hand would turn against the living man, and would measure out to him that measure which he should have measured out to the Macfies."

"This is a queer story." I felt that it was. "But the queerest part is still to come. I am informed, on creditable authority, that the hand was never embalmed. That nothing has been done to preserve it, of any sort or kind. That it has continued, uninterruptedly, in the possession of the Wishaws. And that, after the passage of the centuries, it still looks as fresh and as lifelike as if its original owner still had it, in the proper place, at the end of her arm."

As to the truth of this portion of his story, touching the appearance of life which the hand possessed, I could have gone to the cabinet, taken out its contents, and given him the proof on the spot; and I may add, that I should have done it, had it not been that a contraction of the muscles of my throat seemed to keep me a fixture in my chair.

"Pugh, I mean to see that hand." He should have seen it, then and there, had not the sensation of which I had suddenly become conscious almost amounted to strangulation. "It strikes me that there's a clear case for the Psychical Research Society at last. I have chanced, almost by accident, upon some extraordinary stories of Lady Wishaw's hand. It seems that the Wishaws did keep on killing the Macfies. But they were a prolific breed. As soon as a sire was struck down a son sprang up. There came a time when murder, even in Scotland, was not looked upon with such lenient eyes. Still the Wishaws pursued the even tenor of their way. More than one of them has brought himself within the clutches, and has suffered the last penalties of the law. Finally, even the Wishaws succumbed to the influence of the new spirit of the newer age. They declined to keep on murdering. In fact, they ceased to murder. When they ceased, the hand—the dead hand—Lady Wishaw's hand, began. Pugh, I have reason to believe that, literally, for generations, the head of the family, for the time being, has been found strangled in his bed."

Brasher paused. He stood in front of me with a dramatic gesture. With an effort I found myself able to speak.

"Where did you get that piece of information from, may I inquire?"

"Never mind where I got it from, it is so. You may take it from me that the thing was kept hushed up. It was given out that they died from a spasmodic affection of the heart. Nothing of the kind. There never was a Wishaw with a weak heart yet. At last, only two of them were left, Colin Wishaw, the head of the house, and David, his younger brother. Colin was something like a madman." From the little I had seen of him he had struck me as being about as mad as a man could be, without being pronounced, legally and medically, insane. "He swore a great oath that he would rid himself and the family of Lady Wishaw's hand."

"If what you have told me is correct, Brasher, I fail to see any signs of madness in his doing that."

"The extraordinary part of the thing was the way in which he set himself to carry out his oath. He put the hand in a coffin and buried it, coffin and all. Lady Wishaw's hand returned to him from the grave."

"Oh, Brasher, come!"

"So I am told. He took it with him across the Atlantic. In mid-ocean he dropped it into the sea. When he reached his hotel in New York he found it at his bedside in the morning. He cast it into a smelter's furnace. It was waiting for him when he got home. I am credibly assured that he cooked it and ate it, only to find it on his pillow when he went to bed."

"Brasher, your story begins to remind me of a poem which I read in my childhood days, which, if I remember rightly, was called, and appropriately, called, 'A Horrible Tale'."

"Wait a bit. About a fortnight ago Colin Wishaw was found dead in his bed. There was no mistake about it this time—he had been strangled. It was impossible to hush it up. An inquest was held. The verdict was, that he had been strangled by some person or persons unknown."

If that were so, what on earth did David Wishaw mean by saying that, almost with his last breath, Colin had bequeathed, what appeared to be, *par excellence*, the heirloom of the Wishaws, as a legacy to me. Mr. David Wishaw was a nice man, upon my word!

"The present possessor of Lady Wishaw's hand," continued Brasher, "is David Wishaw, the last living representative of the Wishaw strain." Was he? He would very soon be the possessor, though he was not then. "I am going to call on Mr. David Wishaw. I shall request him to allow me to examine the hand. I intend to make inquiries as to the truth of its extraordinary history. As I have told you, I have reason to believe that its truth will be made quite plain. Should that be so, I shall present the case for the immediate consideration of the Psychical Research Society. I think you will agree with me that a more remarkable case will hardly come its way."

I quite agreed that, if—that little if—he could find evidence to prove it, it would be a remarkable case. And I was more than once on the point of informing him that, if he really desired to look at, and to examine Lady Wishaw's hand he need go no further than where he stood. But each time, as the words had already almost escaped my lips, I again became conscious of what I can only describe as that curious and distinctly involuntary suppression of the larynx.

CHAPTER III

THE HORROR

When Martin Brasher went, he left, so to speak, his story behind. I heartily wished he had not. His story might sound incredible. It might even sound absurd. But there are men, sane men, who are entirely of opinion that it is quite within the bounds of reason to suppose that there may be what the world commonly calls spiritual manifestations—dealings between the seen and the unseen. Of such men, I avowedly, am one. And the idea that there had come to me, from such a deathbed as Colin Wishaw's appeared to have been, a gift which was, in itself, a ghastly gift, and with which was associated such a history—the mere idea to me was full of horror.

Besides, what had prevented me from speaking? What was it that had caused that sensation of pressure about the region of my throat, and so stayed me from telling Brasher that the thing for which he was about to seek, all the time, was at his side, within reach of his arm? What had pinched Nalder? It was a ridiculous inquiry, perhaps—but what had? What had scratched Brasher's face? What had caused the open hand to shut up into a clenched fist, before my very eyes? Was it because the hand, though dead, was living, and was still attached to a living form, though unseen?

Men are made in different fashions. Some men would have found in my situation nothing but pleasurable excitement. For my part I sat in my chair and sweated. I was unwilling to be left alone in my own drawing-room, even though it was broad day. Nothing but shame prevented me from summoning Nalder to come and keep me company. On one point I was resolved, that Lady Wishaw's hand would not remain in my possession. For two hours I endeavoured to summon up sufficient resolution to enable me to rise from my chair, and to go to the cabinet, and to take out the hand, and to pack it up, and to return it whence it came. As I look back upon those two hours, I am half inclined to wonder how it was that, as they have it in the nightmare stories, during their passage my hair did not turn grey. All the while I had the consciousness that something was in the room with me. Something seemed to keep stroking the back of my hand, something with the delicate touch of a dainty woman. I knew that the starch was coming out of my linen. I felt that my collar was becoming as limp as a rag. At last, with what, positively, amounted to a frenzied effort, I sprang from my seat, rushed to the cabinet, opened it, and reached out for the hand, and found that it was—not there.

There could be no question as to whether its apparent disappearance was not one of the effects of being endowed with too vivid an imagination. In the papers in which I had hastily wrapped Lady Wishaw's hand, before going down to lunch, there was nothing at all. "Nalder! Nalder!"

I scarcely think that I expected him to hear me call. I am under the impression that I hardly spoke above a whisper. I began to stagger toward the door, intending to go out on to the landing and call him loudly. As I turned, something was placed against my mouth. Something which felt like the slender fingers of a woman's hand. And my lips were sealed!

CHAPTER IV

WHAT HAPPENED AT THE CLUB

I dined at the club. I am unable to say how I reached it. I know that I did reach it. For me, at least, that is sufficient. I had a little table at the third window from the door. Perkins was my waiter. Perkins is not only an excellent waiter; he is, what is almost of as much importance, an excellent man. I am persuaded that Perkins and I have many things in common. He knows exactly what I like and how I like it. When he tells me what to eat, I eat it, without so much as a hint of an amendment. Never yet have I found that the house of my confidence has been builded on the sand.

I remember that, on that particular night, I had one of the finest woodcocks I ever tasted. Plain roast. I am almost inclined to believe that Perkins must have raised that bird himself, have shot it himself, have hung it himself, and have cooked it himself, he had its history so completely at his finger-ends. Brasher's story, and my two hours' agony, had almost faded from my mind. I do not say that the woodcock was wholly responsible, but it had certainly borne its part. I was just going to drink my second glass of champagne—I don't care what anybody says, everybody has his own taste, and with woodcock I like champagne. I daresay, in another half minute, I should have thanked God that I was alive. The glass was still on its way to my lips when, without any sort of a warning, in an instant, there returned to me that hideous consciousness which had been with me in the afternoon, that something was in the room. I do not mean the waiters, or the diners, and that sort of thing. I wish I did. I mean something intangible, unseen.

I put down my untasted glass. A cold shiver went over me. Then I began to perspire. My feeling was one of the acutest misery. My first impulse, in spite of the woodcock, was to wish that I was dead. In that brilliantly-lighted room, with all the people about me, I was afraid. Perkins was at my side. He had his back to me, for some cause or other, at the moment. All at once he faced round to me, with quite a little twirl. To be frank it was not the kind of movement which was becoming to Perkins. One of his great charms is that he never evinces what I consider indecorous signs of haste. Of an actual twirl, as if he had been a sort of human teetotum, I do not think that he had ever been guilty before.

"I beg your pardon, sir?"

I have no doubt that I looked at him with what were a lack-lustre pair of eyes. I believe that I murmured "Eh?"

"Did you touch me, sir?"

"Touch you? What do you mean?"

"I really must ask you to excuse me, sir,"—Perkins is an educated man—"but I certainly was under the impression, sir, that you pulled my coat-tails."

I pulled his coat-tails! A waiter's! I had, after all, over-estimated Perkins' intellectual powers, if he could suppose that I could be capable of such an action as that. But I said nothing. I rose from the table there and then, and went away. I daresay that Perkins imagined I was bitterly offended. I should certainly have been justified in being so. Or, perhaps, he imagined that I had suddenly gone mad. I left my second glass of champagne untasted. I did not wait for the sweets—Perkins has an exquisite taste in sweets. His sweets never give me indigestion. I said nothing about his wife. (I always inquire after Perkins' wife—who I understand is paralysed, and as good as dead—when he has seen that I have had a creditable dinner.) I went into the smoking-room. I do not know why. I was in no mood to smoke. I take it that I went there simply because, with that intangible unseen something keeping me company, I could not go home.

Several men were in the smoking-room. Tolerably comfortable they seemed, as for a second, I stood at the door and looked round. I envied them. Their contentment with the position in life in which they found themselves placed was so transparently greater than mine. My moving to a seat seemed to create a slight sensation. Each man, as I passed him, gave a perceptible start. Again, I don't know why, I had scarcely seated myself before I became aware that something curious was going on. I seemed to have brought with me an element of discord into the room. Those who had seemed so wholly at their ease, as I viewed them from the door, seemed, all at once, to have been attacked by a fit of the fidgets. A most pronounced fit of the fidgets, too. The attack seemed to be passing from one smoker to the other, right round the room. Under cover of an evening paper I pretended to notice nothing. But I did. Man after man sprang up in his seat and looked about him with an air of startled surprise. Pranklyn was sitting in front of me. "Plain" Pranklyn, as they call him, to distinguish him from the other Pranklyn—"Picture" Pranklyn—who has a chamber of horrors which he calls his picture gallery. Plain Pranklyn is in his seventies, and would turn the scale, I daresay, at eighteen stone. So when I say that suddenly he sprang up from his seat, as if he had been an india-rubber ball, I am aware that the language which I use is strong.

"Good God!" he exclaimed.

Everybody looked at him. All the room was in a stir.

"What is up, Pranklyn?" asked Sir Gerald Carr.

"Who was that caught hold of my hand?"

"Caught hold of your hand? What do you mean?"

"Hanged if I know what I do mean." Pranklyn looked to me as if he were on the verge of an apoplectic fit. "I know that some one caught hold of my hand and twisted it right round."

A man whom I don't know spoke next:—

"That's odd. A moment before some one, or something, did exactly the same thing to me."

"Be George!" cried old Jack Brett. "But there's the devil in the room. I'll swear that some one nearly pulled me hand clean off me wrist."

"And mine!" "And mine!"

Nearly every person present claimed to have undergone a similar experience. There were a score of men turning the smoking-room into a Bedlam. I don't know what the committee would have said. I, for my part, sat as if I were glued to my chair. For, directly Pranklyn sprang from his seat, I felt a hand steal into mine, and fingers and a thumb clasp it about.

"Holloa," said Carr, "what's gone wrong with you? You don't look well."

I rose from my seat with a palsied start. As I did so, the hand let go.

"I'm not feeling well. I—I think that I'll go home." I went home, there and then. As I moved across the room, every man jack of them followed me with his eyes. I don't know if they thought that I had bewitched them, or played some hanky-panky trick. They looked as if they did.

As I went along the passage, and down the steps, into the street, I felt some one twitching at my coat sleeve. I hailed a cab. I bade the cabman drive me home. All the time, as he drove me through the streets, I felt as if there were some one seated beside me in the cab. Some one who continually twitched me by the arm. I doubt if there was ever a sane creature in such a state of mind as I then was. Nalder let me in. He started when he saw my face.

"I hope, sir, you are not ill?"

"To tell the truth, Nalder, I'm not feeling quite the thing. I think I'll have some brandy in my bedroom and go to bed."

I had the strongest reluctance to go, unaccompanied, up my own staircase. I hung about in the hall until Nalder appeared with some brandy on a tray. Together we went up, he in front and I behind. I don't know what he thought of me. He is too well-trained a servant to betray his feelings in his face. At the same time, he is possessed of too much discernment to have failed to see that my indisposition was of a peculiar kind. Especially when, under one pretext and another, I kept him in my bedroom until I was actually between the sheets in bed.

"Shall I leave the light burning, sir?"

It is a peculiarity of mine that I never can sleep where there is a light in the room. On that occasion my choice seemed to lie between the devil and the deep sea. The idea of being left in the dark filled me with a paralysis of horror. On the other hand, what might I not be destined to witness, if the room was light. I chose, mechanically, what I could only hope would turn out to be the less evil of the two.

"Leave it burning. If I find that it keeps me from sleeping, I will get out of bed and put it out."

I did not get out of bed to put it out. Queerly enough, scarcely had Nalder turned his back, than I fell asleep. I must have done, because I remember nothing after he left the room. Nothing, that is, until I awoke. I was not troubled with a dream. I must have slept the quiet dreamless sleep of tired childhood.

CHAPTER V

THE COMING OF THE GIFT

What woke me I do not know, even to this hour. I know that I did wake, to find myself in a cold sweat of agony. Quivering under the overwhelming burden of some unknown horror. For some moments I was only conscious that the room was still lighted. At first, I seemed to have to gasp for breath. But, by degrees, the curtain of unconsciousness was partly lifted, and I became aware that something was with me in the room. What it was, I cannot say. It was something which touched me on the brow. With a light touch, such as we might use to waken a sleeper out of sleep. Only that touch was like the touch of death. I believe that it was the touch of death. Light though it was, under it I could not move. While it remained, I doubt if I breathed. I lay, as I have said, in a cold sweat of agony. When the touch was removed, I closed my eyes. I was afraid of what it was I might see. For what was a period of a few moments I suppose, nothing happened; though I never for an instant lost consciousness of the presence which was with me in the room. As I lay with my eyes fast closed, in agony, something—something tangible—fell on my cheek from above. It had something of the effect of an electric shock. With what I apprehend was an involuntary tension of the muscles of my body, I leaped out of bed on to the floor. I believe that, as I stood on the floor, I cried. Then I stretched out my arms on either side of me, as a blind man might do. Then, and only then, I opened my eyes and looked and saw. Leaning over the bed, I saw that on the pillow on which my head had just been lying was a ring.

I never had a moment's doubt as to the ring's identity. Having seen it once, it was one which I never could forget. It was the ring which had been on the forefinger of the hand which, according to David Wishaw, his brother Colin had bequeathed me as a legacy. The ring which the dead hand had seemed to resent my attempting to remove from its place by clenching itself into a fist. Was it possible that it was offered me as a present after all? Then, by whom? As the scriptural writers have it, my heart melted within me as I realised that it was an offering from the presence which was with me in the room.

I shrunk away. I extended my arms as if to prevent the ring from coming to closer quarters. As I did so I saw a hand advancing across the pillows from the opposite side of the bed. It was the hand which, having once been seen under such circumstances as I had seen it, was no more to be mistaken than the ring. It was, indeed, the hand to which it belonged. The hand of which Brasher had told such a horrible tale. The hand which according to him had urged to murder through the centuries, and then, when its urging had failed, had murdered on its own account.

I saw the hand coming slowly across the bed. It at no time touched the pillow, but, without any visible support, was in the air at a distance above the pillow, of, perhaps, a couple of inches. I saw the dainty fingers close upon the ring. When I saw that, with a spasmodic effort I turned my face away. My glance fell upon the clock which was on the mantelshelf. I noticed, with a singular degree of vividness that, according to that clock, the time was five and twenty minutes to four.

A touch came on my arm. I started round. In front of me was the hand. It was palm uppermost. On the open palm was the ring. It was being held out for me to take. But I would have none of it—although the chance of becoming the possessor of so genuine and unique a curio was hardly likely ever to come again in my way. I slunk back. The hand followed me. It moved quicker than I did. It caught me by the hand. It pressed the ring against my palm. But still I would have none of it. I made no attempt to close my hand so as to retain the ring within my grasp. Suddenly the something which guided and ruled the hand—never, as I have said, for a moment did I lack consciousness of the something which was there—suddenly this something seemed to become annoyed. My persistent, automatic refusal of the proffered ring seemed, in some fantastic way, to give annoyance. All at once, the hand was withdrawn. It was clenched. It was held before me in the air. I saw the ring between the little dainty fingers. Then, with an extraordinary degree of violence, it was thrown against my face.

CHAPTER VI

THE PASSING OF DAVID WISHAW

"Why are you lying there upon the floor?"

It was Brasher's voice. I found, as he said, that I was lying in my night-shirt on the floor. I sat up. I saw that the light still burned.

"Has it gone?"

"Has what gone? What has happened to your face?"

I put my hand up to my face. When I removed it, it was dabbled with blood. It all came back to me—the extreme violence of the movement with which the hand had hurled the ring at me through the air.

"The ring!" was all I said.

"The ring? What ring?" I rose to my feet. I dimly perceived that, for some cause, Brasher was almost as much disturbed as I myself.

We looked each other in the face. "Pugh!" He caught me by the arm. His hand was shaking. "Where is Lady Wishaw's hand?"

I looked around the room. "Is it still here?"

"Here? Where? For God's sake don't speak like that. Your voice is as hoarse as a crow's."

I felt him shiver.

"Why did you not tell me, yesterday, that you were the present fortu-nate possessor of Lady Wishaw's hand?"

I said nothing. He went on. Owing to his haste, or. to some other cause, he seemed to pronounce his words as if he were temporarily afflicted with an impediment in his speech.

"It's been at its devil's tricks again. I've come straight from Wishaw's. David's dead."

"Dead! David Wishaw! Brasher!"

"Don't look at me like that. You look at me as if you were looking at a ghost." Taking out his handkerchief, he wiped his brow. "Yes, David Wishaw's dead. He was the last of the breed. With him all of them have gone. It seems that this morning at a quarter after three—"

"When?"

"This morning, at a quarter after three, his servants heard him scream-ing in his room. When they went to his aid, they could not get to him, because the door was locked. They heard him fighting and yelling within. They called to him but could get no answer. All was still when the shriek-ing ceased. They found the door open. They found him dead. He had been strangled. He was a strong man. He must have fought furiously for his life, because they found him lying in a hideous heap on his bed."

"Brasher, Lady Wishaw's hand was with me here at five and twenty minutes to four."

"Pugh." His jaw dropped down.

"Yes, Brasher, it was here, with me."

"Are you sure that you are not mistaken?"

"And because I would not have the ring, which it endeavoured to force on my acceptance, it flung it in my face with such violence that it cut my face right open, as you see. I wonder if that ring is anywhere upon the floor."

No. We searched everywhere. But it was nowhere to be found. After all, the hand had vanished with that ancient gewgaw of a ring. Acting up to the legend which seemed to me to have been inscribed upon it Lady Wishaw's hand had taken its own.

THE ADVENTURE OF THE
GREAT AUK'S EGG

(MR. TRESS TELLS THE STORY)

CHAPTER I

THE ONE EGG

I am aware that what I will call the story of the Great Auk's egg has been told to the apparent disadvantage of my character. But appearances in this case are misleading. Only the voice of malevolence can suggest that I am capable of conduct to which even the most scrupulous moralist could take exception. Besides, what if I am? Theory is one thing, practice is another. I maintain unhesitatingly that, in one respect, collectors are as alike each other as peas; they are all, with one accord, willing to strain a point—indeed, sometimes several points—if they see a fair chance of adding to their collections.

The committee of the Society of Dilettanti were coming to my place to lunch; the society is now extinct. The affair of the Great Auk's egg may have had something to do with the matter, but, even if it had, I was not the only person who was concerned in that. Indeed, in any case I fail to see that the society was much of a loss. There were not many members—less than a dozen—and most of them were on the committee. Dilettanti, they called themselves; what sort of dilettanti they were my tale will show. It is true that I myself was a member, but then I was asked to join; and anyhow, every man is entitled to make at least one error in the course of his life.

The day before the lunch came off, a man came to me who said his name was Jo Daniels, and who wanted to sell me a Great Auk's egg. I know nothing about eggs; I never pretended to. The egg was a big egg. I knew enough to know that it was not an ostrich's egg. The fellow had a book with him in which were coloured plates; one of the plates purported to represent an egg of the Great Auk. That the man's egg was twin-brother to the egg there represented, seemed to me—who am avowedly not an authority on such a subject—as plain as anything very well could be. I gave him a pound down; I told him that I would inquire into the genuineness of the thing, and, if it turned out all right, if he came again I would give him another. Not a large price to pay for a Great Auk's egg? I never said that it was; I am not in the habit of paying a large price for anything, if I can help it. And when I am told, as I have been told since that little transaction took place, that for a man to give a very little for something worth a very great deal causes his action to wear an aspect of shadiness, all I can reply is that I never knew a collector who would not be willing to pick up a Rembrandt, worth, say, seventy thousand pounds, any day you like for fifty shillings. Yes, and glory in his action, too! Besides, I do not mind confessing that I know no more about the value of a Great Auk's egg than I know about the Great Auk itself. I have heard, or, more probably, I have read, that such a bird existed once upon a time: that is literally all I know about it. Of course, all the men who were coming called themselves collectors. You should see some of their collections! Some of them remind me of the contents of a "marine store" more than of anything else I know; for once in a way they would have a chance of seeing what a collection might be like—in competent hands. Most of them had been to my house before; and though it is true that one never does grow tired of looking at and examining really genuine and intrinsically valuable curios, still I felt that a novelty might not be amiss—even if it only served to increase their ordinary natural sense of jealousy. A few days before I had bought another Bartolozzi—by the way if my action in the matter of the Great Auk's egg looked shady, how about the Bartolozzi?—I never heard a word breathed against me there. Yet I had picked up for five shillings a framed print of Bartolozzi's, which you would be lucky to purchase at any auction-room in London for a five-pound note. I stood the Bartolozzi on a sideboard, leaning against the wall; behind it, between it and the wall, I placed the egg; the print concealed the egg. My idea was to make them green with envy by showing them the print, and then to make them greener by taking away the print and disclosing the egg.

CHAPTER II

THE SEVEN EGGS

Clutton was the first to arrive—Robert Clutton. He is a man of whom I know little, but what little I do know I do not much like. His chief glory is that, sometime before the flood, he wrote—or got somebody to write for him—what he, or somebody else, calls: *A Monograph on the Fossils of Beachy Head.* If he had it announced on the title-page that it was by one of them, he would have been sufficiently near the mark. Pugh came close upon his heels; Pugh I have known for years—and wish I hadn't. He is a man who, under the cloak of virtue, conceals all the vices of which (in)humanity is capable. I could tell tales of Pugh—but there! He began prosing about something or other, I have not the remotest notion what; never was there such a proser! It was some time before Clutton could get a word in, even edgeways; when he got his chance he looked at me in that fatuous way which is a characteristic of his.

"You will be sorry, Mr. Tress, to hear that I have suffered a loss—a very serious loss indeed."

"I hope," I said, "that you have lost nothing from your—collection?"

His collection! You should see it!—I have—and survive! It contains the pen with which somebody signed the Treaty of Amiens, and one of the shoes which Charles I. wore as he mounted the scaffold, and that sort of thing—"real relics" which are "made in Germany" by the gross. He began to yarn.

"About a week ago a person came to me and offered me an article which, with what is acknowledged to be the eye of a connoisseur, I at once perceived was of great and, indeed, unique rarity."

"Was it Cinderella's slipper?"

"No!"—I doubt if Clutton would recognise irony even if you broke his head with it—"it was something which, to the true connoisseur, was of much greater interest than—Cinderella's slipper. It was a whisper from the æons."

"It was a what?"

"I need scarcely say that I speak metaphorically. Though, after all, I do not know why I should call it metaphor. Because it was, in simple truth, and as a statement of absolute fact, a whisper from the æons."

"Did you say that a man brought it with him?"

"He did."

"Have you it in your pocket now?"

"Mr. Tress, you seem to think I am indulging in some foolish jest. I never jest." I believed him; he never does—consciously. "I call it a whisper from the æons because it was a relic of the extinct ages; of a world which is no more; what one might call a vestige of creation."

"We are all vestiges of creation," I ventured to murmur. I felt that, at any rate, Clutton was.

"No doubt, in a sense, we are, but that—that is not the sense in which I use the word. You will be better able to realise what that sense is when I tell you that the article which I was offered was no less than an egg of that extinct aquatic bird, the Great Auk."

Directly he mentioned the name, my thoughts flew to the egg which was behind the Bartolozzi. It occurred to me that it was just as well I had not mentioned it until I had given Clutton an opportunity to tell his little story. "Did you buy it?"

"Was it likely that I should allow such an opportunity to escape me?—one which would scarcely occur again. Mr. Tress, you misjudge me."

"What did you give for it?"

"You must excuse my saying that that is not material. I make it a rule never to mention prices."

Then I knew that he had probably not given my two pounds. "What was the man's name from whom you bought it?"

"His name was Daniels—Jo Daniels." I turned away; I had to. I wondered if Mr. Daniels was a wholesale dealer in Great Auk's eggs. "I suppose the egg was genuine?"

"Undoubtedly. On that I will stake my reputation; and when I say that I will stake my reputation, you know what I mean."

I did. Did he? I wondered if the Great Auk's egg which was behind the Bartolozzi was equally genuine. Pugh struck in prosily:—

"I have read a great deal about that very interesting creature, the Great Auk, but I have never been so fortunate as to have an opportunity of seeing one of its eggs. May I hope—indeed, I shall hope, Mr. Clutton—that I may one day, and one day ere long, have the pleasure of seeing yours."

"I hope you may, sir; I only hope you may. That is the loss of which I was speaking; it is gone!" (Gone! I wondered where.) "Night before last some miscreant stole it from the bureau in my library. I have one consolation. Such an article can only be of interest to a collector. No honest collector, worthy the name, would think of purchasing it without making the most minute preliminary inquiries into the *bona fides* of the vendor."

I turned round sharply. "Clutton, did you make the most minute preliminary inquiries into the *bona fides* of the vendor?"

He hesitated—I knew he would. Then he wriggled—I had foreseen that too.

"To such an inquiry, I—I trust that—that my reputation is a sufficient answer."

"And what," said Pugh, "might be about the value of a Great Auk's egg?"

"In the open market, you mean. That depends, my dear sir, upon so many things; prices fluctuate, one cannot always find a purchaser. I should say, speaking at a venture, that if one were put up at auction to-morrow, you might expect it to fetch anywhere between a hundred and a thousand pounds!"

I all but jumped. The worst of Clutton is, you never can tell whether he is or is not lying. Anyhow, I wished that I could get Pugh and him out of the room so that I might put the egg in a place of safety before the other fellows came with their prying eyes and poking ways. What an ass I had been to put it behind the Bartolozzi! For some cause or other, Clutton saw fit to begin to cross-examine me.

"Are you an authority on the eggs of the Great Auk, Mr. Tress?"

"I know nothing about them." Nor did I—nor do I to this hour.

"Have you ever seen one?"

"I should not know it even if I did." It was a simple statement of a simple fact. Again I challenge contradiction. Clutton went maundering on.

"I think I may say that my loss is irredeemable. My only hope is that the thief may encounter an honest man. I am sure that if he does I shall quickly find myself in possession of my own again."

Just then Andrew Fletcher came in. Andrew Fletcher is my pet aversion. He is a little, keen, eager man, with a sharpness of vision which makes him seem to look, not so much at a person as right through him. The sort of man who, if he thought that you possessed one of Queen Elizabeth's great toes, would never rest easy in his bed until he himself owned the great toes of all her family. He addressed himself to Clutton—when he had shaken hands with us as if he would have liked to screw those members off at our wrists and pocket them.

"You don't seem well, Mr. Clutton—as though you had lost something."

"I have." Clutton had the air of the chief mourner at a funeral. "I have, Mr. Fletcher. Something which it would be no exaggeration to describe as of even national importance."

"Extraordinary thing!" Fletcher turned to me. "By the way, Tress, you don't happen to have been lately purchasing from some lifelong thief of your acquaintance any unconsidered trifle in the shape of a Great Auk's egg?"

When he asked the question, again I all but jumped. Knowing the man as I did, it almost seemed as if he had seen right through the Bartolozzi to the egg behind. I began to wish that I had dug a hole, and buried it in the cellar.

"Might I ask you, Fletcher, to explain, with such courtesy as you have at your command, exactly what you mean?"

"Mean what I say, my good man; have you lately bought a Great Auk's egg?"

"I have not." I had not: the thing had been left upon approval.

"Quite certain?"

I shirked the question, having no taste for unnecessary prevarication. "Why do you address to me your almost too flattering inquiry?"

"Because I've had one stolen. Man came to me a fortnight ago: called himself Jo Daniels. Had a box tied up in a red cotton handkerchief; opened the box; took out an egg—Great Auk's egg. Bought it. Hadn't had it in the house a week when it was stolen."

I listened to Fletcher with, as the novelists say, emotions which may be more easily imagined than described. Either Mr. Daniels was a dealer in Great Auk's eggs in a large way of business, or he was master of an ingenious method of becoming the possessor of an occasional example. Clutton and Pugh both stared. Clutton, I fancy, with something more than amazement.

"Very odd," said Pugh, with what, for him, was marked dryness. "What did you say, Mr. Clutton, was the name of the person from whom you purchased your Great Auk's egg?"

"What's that?" cried Fletcher, sharp as a razor.

Clutton looked more than ever like the chief mourner at a funeral. "It appears to be a singular coincidence; at first sight a very singular coincidence indeed, but he informed me that his name was Daniels; also Jo. May I ask, Mr. Fletcher, when your loss took place?"

"Yesterday week,"

"And when," asked Pugh, "did you make your purchase, Mr. Clutton?"

"The day after."

"What are you two talking about?" This was Fletcher. Pugh took upon himself to answer.

"As Mr. Clutton says, there appears to have been a very singular coincidence. Yesterday week you lost a Great Auk's egg, which you had purchased from a man named Daniels. The day after Mr. Clutton purchased a Great Auk's egg, also from a man named Daniels."

I thought Fletcher would have assaulted Clutton. Unless I am mistaken, for a moment Clutton thought so too—he looked as though he did. Fletcher, however, contented himself with insulting him.

"Mr. Clutton, a receiver is worse than a thief."

Clutton tried to be dignified.

"Mr. Fletcher, my reputation—"

"Your reputation! Give me back my egg!"

"Under any circumstances that would be impossible."

"Impossible!"

I do not know what Fletcher was going to say; he looked as if he was going to say a good flames. But Pugh interposed to pour oil upon the deal.

"No doubt, Mr. Clutton, as you pointed out was the proper course to pursue under such circumstances, you made the most minute inquiries into the *bona fides* of the vendor."

Clutton's misery just then seemed to be real, and not assumed.

"The fact is, that the man appeared to be so simple, and so unequivocally honest, that I never entertained a suspicion as to the possibility of there being anything wrong; nor, indeed, am I prepared to admit that there was."

"Clutton, I don't want to chop straws with you—give me back my egg."

"What you call your egg, Mr. Fletcher, but which in reality was my egg, is no longer in my possession. I, like you, have been the victim of a thief."

"You?"

Again I do not know what Fletcher was going to say. It was just as well that Pugh prevented his saying it, whatever it was.

"Gently, Fletcher, gently! Not the least odd part of this very odd business is that, just as you entered, Mr. Clutton was complaining that the night before last a Great Auk's egg had been stolen from him. The most pertinent question seems to be, who is the present possessor of the apparently twice-stolen property?"

I heartily wished they would change the subject; few things become so tiresome as to hear them continually harping on the same theme. Fortunately, a diversion was created by the entrance of Albert Clements. I crossed the room to greet him, leaving Clutton and Fletcher at it hammer-and-tongs. I only hoped that they would not come to blows in my house, Fletcher is so excitable. Clements is one of those round, rosy men, who are always smiling, and uttering platitudes about Queen Anne's recent decease, and similar original subjects.

"Very warm, isn't it? How well you are always looking, Mr. Tress! Mr. Fletcher seems to be quite excited."

Pugh came sidling up to us: Pugh is a man who always sidles.

"Mr. Clements, Mr. Fletcher has recently suffered a very severe loss."

"Dear me, is that so? How sad! In that case I can sympathise with Mr. Fletcher—so have I. Three weeks ago I had to endure the loss of something which to me was very precious; yes,—an egg of that extinct aquatic bird, the Great Auk."

Clements made this observation with his stereotyped little simper, but I did not hear him with a simper; nor, I fancy, did Pugh hear him with a simper either. Great Auk's egg seemed to be in the air.

"What," asked Pugh, "did you say you had lost, Mr. Clements?"

"Oh, Mr. Pugh! Oh, Mr. Tress!" Clements went into one of those ecstasies of his which to me always suggest hysterics. "It was so unique a specimen, so instinct with suggestion! It was a precious privilege even to have gazed on it; as one did so one seemed to bridge the endless cycles of the revolving years."

"Yes," cut in Pugh, who—for him—looked quite excited. "But what did you say that you had lost?"

Clements did not seem pleased at the interruption; he probably had meant to maunder on for a good ten minutes.

"I thought, Mr. Pugh, I had told you. I have lost something not only of inestimable rarity, but also and at the same time of inestimable interest." Little Clements heaved a sigh. "For, Mr. Pugh, a felon hand has bereaved me of a Great Auk's egg."

Pugh turned to me.

"Tress, everybody seems to have lost a Great Auk's egg. I suppose you don't happen to have found one?"

There was an air of suspicion in his glance which I disliked. The man is himself capable of such abject meanness, that I should not be surprised to learn that he lives in a chronic state of suspicion even of his mother.

"That, my dear Pugh, was the very question I was about to put to you; you have such a knack of finding things, even before they're lost."

Clements paid no attention to us. He was too much absorbed in the memory of his own misfortune.

"Some three weeks since an honest fellow sought, and, I may add, obtained ingress to my presence." It does me good to hear Clements talk—I always wonder where he gets it from. "He was of simple, even rustic bearing. His name, he said, was Daniels."

"What!" cried Pugh—"Daniels!—Jo?"

Clements is a man who is predestined to suffer interruption his whole life long; no one could hear him to the bitter end and live. He looked at Pugh with simpering amazement.

"It is curious, but unless my memory plays me false I really think that he did mention that his Christian name was Jo."

"Clements, just come here!"

Clements went there. Pugh seized him by the shoulder and dragged him there—that is, he dragged him to where Clutton and Fletcher were still insinuating evil of each other. For my part, I was casting about in my mind for some means of getting the egg from behind the Bartolozzi. I wondered if, under cover of the unparliamentary discussion which I saw was imminent, I might not be able to move the print before the eyes of the squabbling quartette, to throw a handkerchief over the egg and walk off with it, without their having in their excitement the least notion of what it was I was doing. While I watched for a propitious moment, I of course heard the remarks which were being exchanged; they were by no means uttered *sotto voce*.

"Mr. Fletcher," exclaimed Pugh, as he towed the somewhat bewildered Clements to a standstill, "what did you say was the name of the man from whom you purchased that Great Auk's egg?"

"Ask Clutton—he knows." Fletcher glared at Clutton as if he would have liked to beat him. He thrust his head forward with that hawk-like trick he has. "Jo Daniels, wasn't it, Clutton?"

"And, Clutton," said Pugh in his oiliest tones—what a hypocrite that man is—worse than Tartuffe—"what did you say was the name of the man from whom you bought the egg?"

Clutton tried his best to look dignified, but the effort was a failure. Fletcher had taken the starch all out of him.

"Really, I am at a loss to comprehend why Mr. Fletcher should suppose me to be more intimate with the man than himself, though Jo Daniels was the name he gave me."

"Now, Clements!" As Pugh turned to Clements he fixed his spectacles in their place in the middle of his nose—the viper! "What was the name of the man from whom you purchased your Great Auk's egg?"

Clements seemed to be confused, which was not surprising.

"I am at a loss to understand the purport of your reiterated inquiry, Mr. Pugh. I have already told you that he called himself Jo Daniels."

Fletcher almost sprang at him.

"You! Clements! Have you had a finger in the pie? What things men are! How ignorant they are of even rudimental honesty! Clements, give me back my egg!"

This method of address did not tend to lighten Clements' darkness—at least, such did not seem to be the case, judging from the expression of his countenance.

"Gently," said the viper, Pugh, "gently, Mr. Fletcher! When, Mr. Clements, did you make your purchase?"

"Some three weeks back."

"And when did you suffer its loss?"

"It was stolen from me—let me see, yesterday was Thursday—it was stolen from me last Wednesday fortnight."

"And when, Mr. Fletcher"—Pugh turned to him—"did you make your purchase?" Unless I am mistaken, Fletcher went a trifle grey. For the first time since I have had the pleasure of his acquaintance, he seemed to be at a loss for an answer. "Mr. Clutton, did we not understand Mr. Fletcher to say that he made his purchase a fortnight ago yesterday—is that not so?" The viper, Pugh, began to softly rub his hands. "Under those circumstances it would almost seem as if Mr. Fletcher bought his egg the very day after Mr. Clements was so unfortunate as to be robbed of his."

Clutton positively smiled. He wagged his finger in Fletcher's face. He even indulged in what I presume he meant for banter.

"Of course, Fletcher, you inquired into the *bona fides* of the purchase? How odd it is that some men are so ignorant of even the rudiments of honesty! Come, give Clements back his egg."

Fletcher still was speechless.

Clements stared from one to the other with an obviously increasing sense of bewilderment.

"Might I ask some one for an explanation? Really, gentlemen, you must pardon my saying that all that has been said is cloaked for me with mystery."

"Very probably, Mr. Clements, very probably." As he explained, Pugh continued to rub his hands together with an air of profound enjoyment of the situation, for which I could have thrown a book at him. "I will give you the position in a nutshell. It would appear that you were robbed of a Great Auk's egg, which you had purchased from a Mr. Jo Daniels. The day after you were robbed, Mr. Fletcher purchased a Great Auk's egg, also from a Mr. Daniels."

"Dear me! How extremely curious!" A glimmer of light seemed to penetrate the obscurity of Clements' brain. "It would almost seem as if the egg which Mr. Fletcher purchased might have been the egg which had been stolen from me."

"It would almost seem so," Pugh sniggered.

Clements' clearness of vision seemed to increase as he perceived Pugh's snigger. "I really am inclining to the opinion than I am entitled to look for the restoration of my property to you, Mr. Fletcher."

"You may look, but you'll look in vain. A thief came my way. Ask Clutton; he's got it now."

"That," exclaimed Clutton, "is a mis-statement of the fact. As Mr. Fletcher is very well aware, the day before yesterday the egg was stolen from me."

"The question," said Pugh, still with a snigger, "therefore appears to be, who, most recently, has played the honourable *rôle* of receiver to a thief."

In the uproar which ensued—all four of them speaking at the top of their voices, and all four of them at once—I thought that I perceived a not unpromising opportunity to convey the egg to a position of, at any rate comparative, security. I was just about to make a dash at the Bartolozzi, when, as luck would have it, the door was opened and Pristlethwaite was announced. Across the room he came, with his usual hop, skip and jump sort of action. Seizing hold of me, he pulled my arm half out of its socket.

"How do, Tress, old boy!" He put up his eyeglass to stare at the quarrelling quartette. "What's the shindy?" He stood listening. "What's that they're saying about a Great Auk's egg? By the way, do you know that somewhere about a month ago, a fellow calling himself Jo Daniels came to me and offered to sell me a Great Auk's egg? Eh!—hullo! what's the matter?"

A great deal was the matter. Pristlethwaite is not a man who speaks in undertones. On the contrary, he has a pretty trick of shouting. When he whispers, you can hear him half across the town. His voice roared above the hubbub which the four were making. When they heard what he said they were still, and turned, and stared.

The simple truth is—and in its simplicity lies its chiefest charm—that there were nine members, including myself, on the committee of the "Society of Dilettanti." They all of them came to my house to lunch. Seven of them had recently purchased a Great Auk's egg! This turned out to be the case, as, one after the other, they were moved to confession as they entered the room. Not the least singular part of the business was that each of them had purchased his egg from the ubiquitous Jo Daniels. And, to increase the singularity of what already was sufficiently singular, not one of them had been able to retain his purchase in his possession for more than a week. Augustus Nicols had been the first to set the ball of purchase rolling. The egg had been stolen from him upon the Tuesday, and, on the Wednesday immediately following, Ralph Gregory became its purchaser. So it went on all down the line. In the course of seven successive weeks, each member of the committee had had his finger in that Great Auk's egg, excepting Pugh and I. Of course, in my case, what purported to be something of the kind had simply been left in my charge upon approval.

The point of the joke was, that each of these men had supposed himself to be exceptionally shrewd. Each of them, too, had been conscious that he was engaging in a transaction which was by no means free from a suspicion of shadiness. For each of them had been perfectly aware that he was buying, from an entire stranger, what was practically a unique, at what was the merest fraction of its market value. As for Mr. Daniels, one could but suppose that he was a rarely gifted genius. As Pristlethwaite put it:—

"The person who sells the same Great Auk's egg to seven different men in succession, and, to enable him to do so, steals it from each of them in turn, is the sort of person one seldom meets, even in these days, when we are becoming accustomed to having our noses stolen from off our faces." He turned to me. "I say, Tress, according to precedent, it's about time that Mr. Daniels should endeavour to find a temporary home for his egg with another member of the committee; what a joke it would be if, this time, he should pitch on you."

"It would be a joke, wouldn't it?"

Pristlethwaite laughed. So did I, or tried to; though what there was to laugh at was more than I could see. Some men are always on the grin.

"I suppose," said Fletcher in that nasty, aggressive way which is, so to speak, a speciality of his, "we may take it for granted that if the thief Daniels were to offer you his notorious property, before becoming its purchaser you would, under the special circumstances, put yourself in communication with your colleagues on the committee?"

"Certainly, Fletcher, you may take it for granted. I assure you that I have no wish that a man should make a fool of me merely because he happens to have succeeded first of all with you."

"Perhaps, Mr. Tress," said Clements, who had returned to the simpering stage, "you have never seen an egg of the Great Auk. Fortunately I made use of my camera to take a photographic picture of mine before it was snatched from me by felon hands; I will show it you."

He took something from one of his pockets. I was in no mood to listen to a lecture on eggs, or on photography either, from Clements.

"Thank you, Clements; possibly my ignorance is not so dense as you imagine."

Of course Pugh was down on me at once.

"I thought, Tress, that you owned that you would not know a Great Auk's egg even if you saw one?"

For the moment I was without a retort for Pugh; so, to my sorrow, Clements made of me his victim. He thrust his wretched photograph underneath my nose.

"I really think, Mr. Tress, that you had better allow me to show you this, if only to prove to you that I have made greater advances in the photographic art than at one time you ventured to foretell. I do not think that that is a bad photograph, even from the professional point of view. As you are no doubt aware, the egg of the Great Auk is not without some marked peculiarities; you, of course, know that the Great Auk was a bird of distinct, and indeed pronounced, aquatic habits. It was its custom to deposit its ovarious concretions—"

And so on. I am not able to give a verbatim account of what the idiot said; I only know that he treated me to what, I take it for granted, was a hotch-potch of his recollections of an article which he had recently read in some encyclopædia or other. To be completely frank, I could not listen; my nerves were all on edge. I wished to goodness that Bob Haines would come and announce that lunch was ready. The men were all more or less in a state of excitement; their one topic of conversation was that wretched egg. I had committed myself in a certain direction rather more than, under the circumstances, I altogether cared for. If Bob would only summon us to lunch, directly the men were out of the room I might have a chance of securing the egg from the imminent risk of achieving undesirable publicity: otherwise, if lunch was delayed, I foresaw that there might be complications.

My foresight was justified: there were.

Pugh was poking and prying round the room, while Clements still literally held me by the button-hole. I saw that he approached the Bartolozzi; my impulse was to make a dash for it, and, under some pretext or other, to drag him from the point of danger. But I knew the man's attitude of chronic suspicion; I feared that with such an one any sudden action on my part might precipitate the possible catastrophe. While Clements went on, like the brook, for ever, I watched his movements. Pugh is as blind as a bat; he had to lean forward to see what he was looking at. As he did so, he made a remark which was possibly intended for the common benefit. I heard it over all.

"The estimable Tress appears to have become possessed of another imitation of Bartolozzi."

As he spoke, reaching out his arms, lifting the framed print off the sideboard, he brought it to within about an inch of his nose. Simultaneously Pristlethwaite, who is quite as fond of prying as Pugh, made a movement towards him.

"Hullo!" he exclaimed, "what's this?"

"What's what?"

Pugh lowered the frame. Pristlethwaite went still closer.

"I say, it's an egg! Hidden behind the picture!"

It was the egg! Pugh's action in displacing the Bartolozzi had achieved for it that publicity which at the moment I had not desired. Although the fact of my entire freedom from any sort of evil intent was altogether beyond question, although I knew that my motives, in every possible sense, could bear the investigating light of day, still I had hidden it behind the Bartolozzi, and I had not informed the company that it was there. Now Pristlethwaite's words had called general attention to its propinquity. They stared at the egg; then, for some reason, they stared at me. I was speechless. Never in my life did I so nearly lose my presence of mind; indeed, for some moments I believe I lost it. As they looked at me, with what seemed to be their accusatory eyes—men who, from the bottom of my heart, one and all, I cordially despised—something seemed to dry up within me. I doubt if, for some seconds, I could have spoken. I was silent—with the silence of startled innocence.

"So it is! positively—an egg!" Pugh pretended to be surprised into dropping my Bartolozzi from his hands on to the floor. The glass was shivered into fragments. He paid not the slightest attention to the injury which he had done my property. "What an odd place in which to hide an egg: and such a fine egg, too! Tress, you don't look happy. Is it because we have inadvertently spoiled what you intended should be a little surprise? Tress, is this an ostrich's?"

Fletcher rushed forward.

"An ostrich's! It's my Great Auk's!"

He snatched the egg from off the sideboard, he held it above his head.

"Yours!" cried Pristlethwaite. "George, it looks uncommonly like mine."

"Unless I am mistaken," put in Clutton, "it is the one which, the day before yesterday, was stolen from me."

Clements thrust his photograph into the centre of the throng.

"If you will look at this photograph, gentlemen, you will at once perceive it is mine."

And with one accord they laid claim to the egg, clustering about it like a swarm of bees. Pugh alone stood apart.

"Really, Tress," he sniggered, "this does appear to be a morning of coincidences."

Just as I was expecting that, of a certainty, they would destroy the egg between them, Fletcher, forcing his way through the crowd, stood forward, and, with the egg still in his hand, confronted me.

"Mr. Joseph Tress, you are my host: do not let me forget that I am your guest." He turned to the others: "No, gentlemen, under the pressure of any possible combination of circumstances, do not let us forget that we are this gentleman's friends and guests, and his colleagues on the committee."

"That is all very well," cried Pristlethwaite; "but, hang me! if I shouldn't like to have some sort of explanation. Look here, Tress, I'll take my oath that that is the Great Auk's egg which was stolen from me. Perhaps you'll be so good as to explain how it came to be in your room, and hidden behind that picture."

My man Bob appeared at the door; he addressed himself to me:—

"There's a man named Jo Daniels downstairs, who says he wishes to speak to you."

I faced the excited seven.

"Mr. Pristlethwaite and gentlemen, my servant informs me that an individual has just arrived who is more competent to supply you with the explanation which you desire than I am. Bob, show Mr. Daniels upstairs."

CHAPTER III

MR. JO DANIELS EXPLAINS

Mr. Daniels came into the room—or rather, he shambled into the room—with what Clements had called his simple, almost rustic gait. As he entered, he cast a startled glance around; in a moment all the shamble went out of his bearing. If I had not, anticipating his movements, interposed between him and the door, he would have gone out more rapidly than he had entered.

"Well, Mr. Daniels, you have favoured me with the pleasure of a second visit rather sooner than I had expected, and at a most auspicious moment. I suppose you are anxious to know if I have made inquiries into the character of that egg of yours. I have. In consequence of those inquiries, I think I may say that we all of us are glad to see you."

"Trapped!" Mr. Daniels murmured, "s'elp me!"

I went on. "Yesterday, Mr. Daniels, you were so good as to leave a Great Auk's egg with me upon approval. Might I ask you where you got it from?"

"Certingly. Didn't I tell yer?" Mr. Daniels displayed as fine an air of impudence as one might care to see. "I'm a seafaring man, that's what I am, and I brought it back with me on my last woyage to the Sandwich Isles."

This was more than the seven could stand.

"You rascal!" cried Fletcher. "You first of all sold it to, and then stole it from, me!"

"You certainly," said Clutton, "stole it, the day before yesterday, from me."

"I strongly suspect," stormed Clements, "that three weeks ago you stole it from me."

They were all of them at him at once. So far as I could judge, Mr. Daniels never turned a hair.

"It's no good parleying with a scoundrel of this type," shouted Pristlethwaite, probably perceiving that Mr. Daniels was not over-sensitive on his moral side. "Might I trouble you, Tress, to send for the police?"

"Steady!" observed Mr. Daniels, raising his hand as if to allay the storm. He showed no outward signs of discomposure. To me, he seemed to be from every point of view the coolest person in the room. "Half a mo'! Just let me say 'arf a dozen words so that we may know who the police is coming for!" Every trace of simplicity had vanished: his impudence became as voluble as it was plausible. "Now, gents, don't you think you're a little 'ard on me? Ain't you every bit as much upon the cross as me? Didn't you know you was a-buying something for almost nothing, what was worth a 'eap of money? Didn't you think you'd caught a flat, and was a-taking it out of 'im according? I say more. Didn't you more than 'arf guess that there might be something a little bit—you know!—about a chap like me getting 'old of an article like that? As man to man, I say frankly; answer me that!" As he paused for the answer, which did not come, he actually winked at the astounded seven. Drawing himself upright, he assumed a fine air of virtuous indifference. "So far as I'm concerned, whether you send for the police, or whether you don't, it makes no odds to me. Only, when it comes afore the beak, and it turns out that all you gents 'as been a-tryin' to do each other, and that you only went nasty when you found out that a poor, simple bloke like me was a little bit more fly than you quite thought, I shouldn't be surprised if the case made some lively reading in the noospaper, not a bit, I shouldn't."

"The scoundrel's insolence," shouted Pristlethwaite, when the silence was becoming almost painful, "is as colossal as his villainy. Once more, Tress, I ask you to send for the police."

"Softly does it!" Mr. Daniels seemed, if possible, to be more at his ease than ever. "Still 'arf a mo'! Might I ask you, gents, to tell me what you thought you was a-buying?—might I ask you, sir, to tell me what you thinks you're a 'olding in your 'and?"

The latter question was addressed to Andrew Fletcher, who was still retaining in his grasp the object of so much interest. He snapped out a reply:—

"Don't think to play the fool with me, my man! I know quite as well as you do what this is; this is my Great Auk's egg."

Fletcher held it out in front of him, as if daring any one to challenge his rights of ownership. The shameless Mr. Daniels absolutely smiled within a foot or two of Fletcher's angry countenance.

"Oh, it's your Great Auk's egg, is it? Then that's just where you're mistaken, don't you know. Just half a mo'! Before you 'as your say you let me say my say right out. Now, look 'ere gents, I'll just tell you all about it, and that's straight, and nothing couldn't be straighter than that. A pal of mine, he says to me one night as 'ow he knows a lot of toffs what calls theirselves collectors! 'Collectors?' I says. 'What's them?' He says: 'You should see their 'ouses; crammed up with stuff! You never see such rubbish in your life; they spends their lives a-buying it!' 'Well,' I says, 'I don't see what odds that makes to me!' He say: 'Don't you 'urry, Jo! You says you're stony, don't you? Well, I'll put you up 'ow to make a bit out of these 'ere old toffs.' It was in the Borough we was a-talking, one Saturday night. 'See that?' he says. 'See what?' says I. 'Why, this 'ere': with that, he picks up off a barrer—you know what I mean!—one of them pot eggs, made of china— porcelain's what they calls it—only I never see such a big one in all my life, nor yet one 'arf so big. 'I've got a book at home,' says my pal, 'what's got a picture in it of what they calls a Great Auk's egg. These 'ere Great Auk's eggs is worth a mint of money to them as cares for 'em. I'll lend you this 'ere book, and I'll buy you this 'ere egg, Jo'—meaning the pot egg. 'You fake it up like this picture, and you take it to one of these 'ere old toffs what I've been a-telling you about, and you yarn 'im that it's a egg of that there dead-and-gone old rooster what they calls a Great Auk. He'll give yer what yer likes for it, if yer yarns 'im nicely. Why, bless you, Jo,' he says 'if you was to take your Alfred David that it was something that nobody never 'adn't seen afore, these 'ere old toffs they'd buy anything you liked to offer 'em—straight, they would!—s'elp me!' Well, I takes this 'ere pot egg 'ome with me, and I fakes it up like this 'ere picture in this 'ere book—though I never didn't think that nobody never wouldn't be 'ad on such a lay as that.

But, lord love you! when I come to the first old toff—that's 'im, what's a-standing there; ain't yer, sir?"

Mr. Daniels thrust his cloth cap in the direction of Augustus Nicols. Mr. Nicols suddenly evinced an unexpected inclination to conceal his corpore-ality behind the persons of his colleagues.

"Why," continued Mr. Daniels, "talk of the innocence of the sucking-dove, let alone a blooming baby, nothing of that sort never wasn't in it alongside of this 'ere old toff, now was it, sir? All he thought about was a-doing me; and, my crikey, he done me prime! He got this 'ere Great Auk's egg out o' me for a bit of money what was such a little bit, it'd 'ave made the downiest old fence ever yet I 'eard of see stars. Now, didn't you, sir? I ask you that!"

"You abominable vagabond!" murmured Mr. Nicols, as he wiped the moisture from his brow.

"And what I says is this: send for the police if you like, don't mind me! But, mark my words, as I said afore, when it comes afore the beak, and it turns out that you gents 'as been a-trying to cut each other's throats, and a-playing it low down, all on account of a pot egg what a pal o' mine picked up for ninepence off a barrer in the Borough, let alone it's making some lively reading in the noos-papers, I wouldn't be surprised if it was mentioned in the comics, too."

Silence, which, as somebody has expressed it, might have been felt, ensued. For my part, I never have pretended to be a judge of eggs. On the contrary, I have stated over and over again that I know nothing at all about them; at the same time, I am bound to affirm that I had felt that there was something curious about his egg the moment Mr. Daniels had placed it in my hand. As regards his dupes, I have never entertained any delusions on the subject of their intelligence, or want of it: their crass imbecility in no way took me by surprise. None the less, they had my sympathy. So far as Pugh was concerned, they did not receive from him even that. I had no-ticed him listening to Mr. Daniels' little narrative with a smile of obviously increasing enjoyment. When no one evinced a pressing desire to carry the conversation further, he advanced to Fletcher.

"Might I ask you, Mr. Fletcher, to allow me to examine this interesting relic of the ages which are no more?"

The readiness with which Fletcher suffered Pugh to take the egg away from him was in marked contrast to his previous desire to retain it, at any cost, in his possession.

"So this is the egg of that extinct aquatic bird, the Great Auk. As we look at it, as has been said in finer phrases than I can claim to have at my command how our thoughts bridge the ages which are gone. I observe that it has a hole at either end: it is at least so much an egg as that."

"Yes," said Mr. Daniels, "my pal, he says to me, 'make a couple of peep-holes in it, Jo, so that these 'ere old toffs shall think as it's been blowed'."

"Beautiful! beautiful!" Balancing the egg on the tips of the fingers of one hand, Pugh gazed at it with what he possibly desired us to believe was admiration. He tapped it with a metal pencil-case. "China—real china—there cannot be a doubt of it! without even the suspicion of a crack: an excellent example of its kind!"

"So," said Mr. Daniels, "it ought to be—for ninepence."

Pugh turned to the seven.

"I hope—without, I confess, entertaining any very fervent belief that my hope will be realised—that this will be a lesson to you, my friends. You will allow that, on previous occasions, I have pointed out to you that it is mere perversity of folly for ignorance to pretend to knowledge. How often have I hinted, with what was the solicitude of a true friend, that the half, it may be three-quarters—it may be, indeed, the whole, of what you call your collections, may consist, for all you know, as our friend—or, rather, your friend—Mr. Daniels has expressed it, of the most utter rubbish. The fact is—and facts are stubborn things—that for men of your particular mental calibre—"

I interposed. It occurred to me that if Pugh continued his remarks to the end there might be friction. Going forward, I drew the men aside; I hinted that, under the peculiar circumstances of the case, it might perhaps be just as well if, showing mercy, we did not press the matter to a prosecution, and did not urge the law to inflict on the ingenious Mr. Daniels that punishment which he had so righteously deserved. I was about to suggest that we might leave him to his own conscience, when Pugh interrupted me.

"If you are suggesting, my dear Tress, that Mr. Daniels may be allowed to go, you may save yourself that trouble. He has gone."

He had. The shifty scamp had taken advantage of my leaving the door for a moment to slip through it, and make a dash for liberty. Even as my attention was called to the fact, we heard the front door slam. Almost simultaneously my man Bob came in.

"Lunch," he said, "is served."

So, as in all human probability Mr. Daniels had already vanished round the corner of the street, we went downstairs to lunch.

www.ingramcontent.com/pod-product-compliance
Lightning Source LLC
Chambersburg PA
CBHW020656180626
46816CB00003B/1315

9781479471041